Thomas Warton

The Oxford sausage

Select poetical pieces

Thomas Warton

The Oxford sausage
Select poetical pieces

ISBN/EAN: 9783337278700

Printed in Europe, USA, Canada, Australia, Japan

Cover: Foto ©Andreas Hilbeck / pixelio.de

More available books at **www.hansebooks.com**

THE

OXFORD SAUSAGE:

OR,

SELECT POETICAL PIECES,

Written by the moſt

CELEBRATED WITS

OF THE

UNIVERSITY OF OXFORD.

A NEW EDITION.

Adorned with CUTS, Engraved in a NEW TASTE, and Deſigned by the BEST MASTERS.

——— *Tota, merum Sal.*　　　LUCR. iv. 1156.

O X F O R D:

Printed for G. ROBINSON, in *Pater-noſter-Row*, and F. NEWBERY, the Corner of *St. Paul's Church-Yard, London*; W. JACKSON and J. LISTER, in *Oxford*; and ſold by the Bookſellers of *Oxford* and *Cambridge*.

M.DCC.LXXVII.

[Price Two Shillings, ſewed.]

PREFACE.

THE Plan of the following Miscellany may justly be considered as entirely new. Our Design was to form a Collection of such small, but valuable, *Poetical Pieces*, written by Gentlemen of OXFORD, as never before appeared together; and which being hitherto published separately, or, as it were, by Accident, would otherwise have been overlooked and forgotten, partly for want of Length, and partly from their Manner of Publication. Amongst these, are interspersed several Pieces of

the

the greateſt Merit, never before printed. This Stock of Materials, which All will allow to be *highly ſeaſoned,* thus carefully ſelected, and happily blended, we have ventured, with ſome Degree of Propriety, to preſent to the Public, under the Name of The Oxford Sausage.

Our principal Aim, has been to collect Poems of *Humour* and *Burleſque.* And in Conformity to this Intention, our *Cuts,* for which the moſt able Maſters have been engaged, are engraven in the ſame Style. On theſe Conſiderations, our Sausage, we preſume, will not only gratify the Palate, but, if the old and approved Proverb, Laugh and be Fat, be true, will, at the ſame Time, contribute to make our Readers *Thrive.* All ſuch Perſons, therefore, as are grown *thin,* by too much Study, Faſting, and

low

low Spirits, if they would improve their Conftitution, and mend their Habit, are hereby invited to partake of this cheap, delicious, and falutary *Morfel.* As to Readers of a more genial Complexion, and a more joyous Difpofition, we need not doubt of being favoured with their Company. In the mean Time it is declared, that we do not mean by our *Title* to exclude any particular Sect or Denomination of People. For *Jews,* as well as *Chriftians,* may feed on our Sausage, without hurting their Confciences.

In order to render the following Mifcellany complete, no Pains have been fpared in procuring Pieces, and no Refources have been left unexplored. That nothing might efcape us, we have even examined the indefatigable Dr. *Rawlinfon's* voluminous Collection of Manu-. fcripts,

A 4

fcripts, lately prefented to the *Bodleian Library*. But, we muft acknowledge, without Succefs; as not one *poignant Ingredient* was to be found in all that immenfe Heap of rare and invaluable *Originals*. Indeed, our chief Affiftance has been from fome curious and ingenious Members of the Univerfity of *Oxford*, who have made it their Bufinefs to preferve fuch *fugitive* Pieces, as were beft *adapted* to this *Defign*.

Many Conjectures, we apprehend, will be formed, concerning the *Collector* of this Work. Some will probably fufpect him to be that *whimfical* Genius who compiled the COMPANION TO THE GUIDE; while Others will perhaps guefs him to be the fame with the *well-bred* and *humourous* Writer of the late TERRÆ FILIUS. But thefe *fagacious Invefligators* will have

found

found out nothing, even if they fhould fucceed thus far in their Conjectures : as moft unluckily the Author of thofe Pieces will never be *known*. Notwithftanding, whoever fhall be fo happy as to make this *Difcovery*, and will, on unqueftionable Proof, deliver in the *Collector*'s REAL Name, to Mr. JACKSON, *Printer, in the High-ftreet, Oxford*, fhall receive, as a Reward for unriddling this Myftery, and on Condition that the *Secret* go no further, *Twelve* SAUSAGES, in *Turkey*, gilt, and lettered.

It may be proper, in this Place, to advertife our Readers, that great Part of the firft Edition of this Work was printed off, when we were fo unfortunate as to lofe the facetious Mr. BENJAMIN TYRRELL, Cook, in the *High-ftreet, Oxford*. But it is hoped that BEN's *Cookery*,

which

which makes no inconfiderable Figure in
this Work, will ftill continue to be *re-
lifhed* by all Readers of true *Tafte*.

It was intended, by Way of Frontif-
piece, to prefix to our firft Edition, an
elegant Engraving of *Mother* SPREAD-
BURY's Head, the original Inventrefs of
the true *Oxford* Saufage.　But as no *ftri-
king* Likenefs of that celebrated *Matron*
could be procured in Time, we were
obliged to defer gratifying the World in
that Particular, till the Publication of
this fecond Impreffion.

CONTENTS.

The

CONTENTS.

On

CONTENTS.

CONTENTS.

V E R S E S

OCCASIONED BY

BEN TYRRELL's MUTTON PIES.

✠✠✠✠✠✠✠✠✠✠✠✠✠✠✠✠✠✠✠✠✠✠✠✠✠✠✠✠✠

ADVERTISEMENT.

ALL ye that love what's *nice* and *rarifh*,
  At *Oxford*, in St. *Mary*'s Parifh,
BEN TYRRELL, Cook of high Renown,
To pleafe the Palates of the *Gown*,
At Three-pence each makes MUTTON-PIES,
Which thus he begs to advertife:
He welcomes all his Friends at *Seven*,
Each *Saturday* and *Wedn'fday* Even *.

 * Mr. TYRRELL, Cook, in the High-ftreet, Oxford, having formed a laudable Defign of obliging the Univerfity with
Mutton-Pies, twice a Week ; this Advertifement appeared,
on that Occafion, in the OXFORD JOURNAL, *November*
25th, 1758.

No Relicks ſtale, with Art unjuſt,
Lurk in Diſguiſe beneath his *Cruſt* ;
His Pies, to give you all fair Play,
Smoak only when 'tis *Market-Day :*
And all muſt own, how *freſh* his Meat,
While JOLLY's Porter crowns the Treat.

    If *Rumps* and *Kidneys* can allure ye,
BEN takes upon him to aſſure ye,
No Cook ſhall better hit the Taſte,
In giving Life and Soul to *Paſte.*
If *cheap* and *good* have Weight with Men,
Come all ye Youths, and ſup with BEN.
If *Liquor* in a MUTTON-PIE
Has any Charms, come taſte and try !
O bear me Witneſs, *Iſis'* Sons !
Pierce but the Cruſt — the *Gravy* runs : —
The Taſter licks his Lips, and cries,
" O RARE BEN TYRRELL'S MUTTON-PIES !"

    But hold — no more — I've ſaid enough —
Or elſe my PIES may prove——a PUFF.

BEN

BEN TYRRELL's, *Wednesday Night,*
December 6th, 1758.

HOW I congratulate fair *Isis,*
 That such the Taste for *Mutton Pies* is!
Hail glorious BEN! whose Genius high
First plann'd a genuine MUTTON-PIE!
Born to combine with matchless Taste,
The Charms of *Pepper* and of *Paste!*
Was but the Motion of my Pen
Quick as thy *Rolling-Pin,* O BEN!
O, could my Thoughts thy Pastry ape,
And slide, like yielding Dough, to Shape;
My Genius, like thy Oven glow,
My Numbers, like thy Gravy flow;
Or, in the Twinkling of an Eye,
I *cook* an *Ode* —— as you a *Pie;*
O then, (nor think, to mock thy Trade,
My Promises of *Pie-Crust* made) ——
I'd raise thy culinary Fame
Above immortal *Spreadbury's* Name:
Though from all Cooks, a Matron wise,
In *Sausages* she bore the Prize:
Her *seasoning* Hand should yield to thine,
Thy *Mutton* should her *Pork* outshine.

       Nor

Nor shall the Muse esteem it Folly,
To blend with thine the Praise of JOLLY *.
Thy lov'd Compeer! cogenial Friend!
Who mild, when Evening Shades descend,
Imparts the froth-crown'd *Porter's* Aid,
To smooth the serious Brow of Trade:
Both shall together mount the Skies,
The PORTER his —— but thine the PIES.

 Thine is the House, dear BEN, to call at,
Or for the *Pocket* or the *Palate*.
For thee, the Citizen and Cit
Their cold boil'd Beef and Carrots quit:
Grave Aldermen, ambitious, share
In *Alma Mater's* classic Fare:
The blooming Toasts of *Oxford* Town
Catch the Contagion of the *Gown*,
And wish the wonted Ev'ning nigh,
'To *have a Finger in the Pie.*
As so *enticing* TYRRELL's House is,
Send not too *late* ye pregnant Spouses!
Think of the Midwife's vast Surprize,
To see Boys *mark'd* with *Mutton Pies!*

 If this the universal Taste is
What will become of *Ven'son Pasties?*

---

* CAPTAIN JOLLY, who, *pro bono Publico*, first reduced
the Price of Porter in Oxford, from 6*d.* to 4*d.* a Quart.

What of the *Cates*, which many a Maiden,
For the next *Chriſtmas* Cheer has laid in ?
Sure all with BEN will ſup and dine,
And leave their CHRISTMAS PIES for THINE.

ΠΙΟΦΙΛΟΣ.

EPIGRAM, *occaſioned by a ſuppoſed extraordinary*
Phænomenon in MIDWIFERY.

I.

SAGE Wooɒs ! though many a Dark Affair
    Be known to thy diſcerning Eyes ;
E'en You, with all your Skill, muſt ſtare,
   " To ſee Boys mark'd with Mutton Pies !"

H. What

II.

What if our *Wives*, with equal Glee,
 In Thought a *Sausage* should enjoy ;
Say, would you wonder much, to see
 The MOTHER's LONGINGS mark the Boy ?

On BEN TYRRELL's *Pies.*

LET *Christmas* boast her customary Treat,
 A Mixture strange, of Suet, Currants, Meat,
Where various Tastes combine, the greasy, and the
  sweet.
Let glad *Shrove-Tuesday* bring the *Pancake* thin,
Or *Fritter* rich, with Apples stor'd within :
On *Easter-Sunday* be the *Pudding* seen,
To which the *Tansey* lends her sober Green :
And when great *London* hails her annual *Lord*,
Let quiv'ring *Custard* crown the *Aldermannic* Board.

 But BEN prepares a more delicious Mess,
Substantial Fare, a Breakfast for Queen *Bess :*
What dainty Epicure, or greedy Glutton,
Would not prefer his PIE, that's made of *Mutton ?*

 Each diff'rent Country boasts a diff'rent Taste,
And owes it's Fame to *Pudding* and to *Paste :*

SQUAB

SQUAB PIE in *Cornwall* only can they make,
In *Norfolk* DUMPLING, and in *Salop* CAKE;
But *Oxford* now from all shall bear the Prize,
Fam'd, as for *Sausages*, for MUTTON-PIES.

MUTTON-PIES *for the* ASSIZES.

March 1, 1760.

BEHOLD, once more, facetious BEN
  Steps from his *Paste* —— to take the *Pen*;
And as the *Trumpets*, shrill and loud,
Precede the Sheriff's *Javelin'd* Crowd,
So BEN before-hand advertises
His snug-laid Scheme for the *Assizes*.
Each of the Evenings, BEN proposes
With PIES so nice to *smoak* your Noses:
No Cost, as heretofore, he grudges,
He'll stand the Test of able JUDGES;
And think, that when the *Hall* is *up*,
How *cheap* a *Juryman* may *Sup*!
For LAWYERS CLERKS, in Wigs so smart,
A tight warm Room is set apart.——
My MASTERS eke, (might BEN advise ye)
Detain'd too long at *Nizey Prizey*,
Your College Commons lost at *Six*,——
At BEN's the *jovial* Evening *fix*;

From

From * *Tripe*-Indentures, ftale and dry,

Efcap'd to PORTER and a PIE.

Hither, if ye have any Tafte,

Ye BOOTED EVIDENCES, hafte!

Ye LASSES too, both tall and flim,

In *Riding Habits* drefs'd fo trim,

Who, ufher'd by fome *Young Attorney*,

Take, each Affize, an *Oxford Journey*:

All, who *fubpœna'd* on th' Occafion,

Require *genteel* Accommodation,

Oh hafte to BEN's, and *fave your Fines*

You'd pay at Houfes deck'd with *Signs!*

Lo I, a Cook of Tafte and Knowledge,

And bred the *Coquus* of a *College*,

Having long known the STUDENT's Bounty.

Now dare to *cater* for the *County*.

    Come then, of BEN, O come, and buy All —

As 'tis *Affize-Time*, he'll ftand *Trial*;

His *Caufe* Succefs will furely crown,

His *Witneffes* —— are ALL the GOWN.

       * I fuppofe BEN means *tripartite*.

    ☞ *Thefe five Pieces are all that appeared on this Subject.*

ODE

ODE *to a* GRIZZLE WIG.

By a Gentleman who had juſt left off his BOB.

ALL hail, ye CURLS, that rang'd in reverend Row,
  With ſnowy Pomp my conſcious Shoulders hide !
That fall *beneath* in venerable *Flow*,
And crown my Brows *above* with *feathery* Pride !

High on your Summit, *Wiſdom*'s mimick'd Air
Sits thron'd, with *Pedantry* her ſolemn Sire,
And in her Net of awe-diffuſing Hair,
Entangles Fools, and bids the Croud admire.

O'er

O'er every Lock, that floats in full Display,
Sage *Ignorance* her Gloom scholaftic throws;
And ftamps o'er all my Vifage, once fo gay,
Unmeaning *Gravity's* ferene Repofe.

Can thus *large Wigs* our Reverence engage?
Have *Barbers* thus the Pow'r to blind our Eyes?
Is Science thus conferr'd on every Sage,
By *Baylifs,* *Blenkinfop,* and lofty *Wife?* *

But thou farewel, my Bob! whofe thin-wove *Thatch*
Was ftor'd with *Quips* and *Cranks,* and *wanton Wiles,*
That *love* to *live* within the one-curl'd *Scratch,*
With *Fun,* and all the Family of *Smiles.*

Safe in thy *Privilege,* near *Ifis'* Brook,
Whole Afternoons at *Wolvercote* I quaff'd;
At Eve my carelefs Round in *High-ftreet* took,
And call'd at JOLLY's for the *cafual* Draught.

No more the *Wherry* feels my Stroke fo true;
At *Skittles,* in a *Grizzle,* can I play?
Woodftock, farewell! and *Wallingford,* adieu!
Where many a *Scheme* reliev'd the lingering Day.

Such were the Joys that once *Hilario* crown'd,
E'er grave *Preferment* came my Peace to rob:
Such are the lefs ambitious Pleafures found
Beneath the *Liceat* of an humble Bob.

* Eminent Peruke-Makers in Oxford.

EPISTLE

E P I S T L E,

From THOMAS HEARN, *Antiquary,*

To the AUTHOR of

The COMPANION *to the* OXFORD GUIDE, *&c.*

FRIEND of the mofs-grown Spire and crumbs
    ling Arch,
Who wont'ſt at Eve to pace the long-loſt Bounds
Of lonefome *Ofeney !* What malignant Fiend
Thy cloyſter-loving Mind from antient Lore
Hath bafe feduc'd ? Urg'd thy apoſtate Pen

To

To trench deep Wounds on *Antiquaries* fage,
And drag the venerable Fathers forth,
Victims to Laughter! Cruel as the Mandate
Of mitred Priefts, who *Baſkett* late enjoin'd
To throw afide the reverend Letters *black*,
And print *Faſt-Prayers* in *modern* Type! — At this
*Leland**, and *Willis*, *Dugdale*, *Tanner*, *Wood*,
Illuftrious Names! with *Camden*, *Aubrey*, *Ll yd*,
Scald their old Cheeks with Tears! For once they hop'd
To feal thee for their own! and fondly deem'd
The Mufes, at thy Call, would crowding come
To deck *Antiquity* with Flowrets gay.

But now may Curfes every Search attend
That feems inviting? May'ft thou pore in vain
For dubious Door-ways! May revengeful Moths
Thy Ledgers eat! May chronologic Spouts
Retain no Cypher legible! May Crypts
Lurk undifcern'd! Nor may'ft thou fpell the Names
Of Saints in ftoried Windows! Nor the Dates
Of Bells difcover! Nor the genuine Site
Of Abbot's Pantries! And may *Godſtowe* veil,
Deep from thy Eyes profane, her *Gothic* Charms!

* Names of eminent Antiquaries.

THE

THE

PROGRESS *of* DISCONTENT.

WRITTEN IN THE YEAR, 1746.

WHEN now, mature in claffic Knowledge,
   The joyful Youth is fent to College,
His Father comes, a Vicar plain,
At Oxford bred——in Anna's Reign,
And thus in Form of humble Suitor,
Bowing, accofts a reverend 'Tutor.

                    " Sir,

" Sir, I'm a Glo'fterfhire Divine,
" And this my eldeft Son of nine;
" My Wife's Ambition and my own
" Was that *this* Child fhould wear a Gown::
" I'll warrant that his good Behav'our
" Will juftify your future Favour;
" And for his Parts, to tell the Truth,
" My Son's a very forward Youth;
" Has Horace all by Heart—you'd wonder—
" And mouths out Homer's Greek like Thunder.
" If you'd examine—and admit him,
" A Scholarfhip would nicely fit him:
" That he fucceeds 'tis ten to one;
" Your Vote and Intereft, Sir!—'Tis done."

Our Pupil's Hopes, though twice defeated,
Are with a Scholarfhip compleated :
A Scholarfhip but half maintains,
And College Rules are heavy Chains :
In Garret dark he fmokes and puns,
A Prey to Difcipline and Duns ;
And now intent on new Defigns,
Sighs for a Fellowfhip——and Fines.

When

When nine full tedious Winters paſt,
That utmoſt Wiſh is crown'd at laſt:
But the rich Prize no ſooner got,
Again he quarrels with his Lot:
" Theſe Fellowſhips are pretty Things,
" We live indeed like petty Kings:
" But who can bear to waſte his whole Age
" Amid the Dullneſs of a College,
" Debarr'd the common Joys of Life,
" And that prime Bliſs — a loving Wife?
" O! what's a Table richly ſpread
" Without a Woman at its Head!
" Would ſome ſnug Benefice but fall,
" Ye Feaſts, ye Dinners! farewel all!
" To Offices I'd bid adieu,
" Of Dean, Vice-præs, — of Burſar too;
" Come Joys, that rural Quiet yields,
" Come Tythe, and Houſe, and fruitful Fields!"

Too fond of Liberty and Eaſe
A Patron's Vanity to pleaſe,
Long Time he watches, and by Stealth,
Each frail Incumbent's doubtful Health;
At length —— and in his fortieth Year,
A Living drops —— two hundred clear!

With Breaſt elate beyond Expreſſion,

He hurries down to take Poſſeſſion.

With Rapture views the ſweet Retreat——

" What a convenient Houſe! how neat!

" For Fuel here's ſufficient Wood :

" Pray God the Cellars may be good !

" The Garden — that muſt be new plann'd ——

" Shall theſe old-faſhion'd Yew-trees ſtand ?

" O'er yonder vacant Plot ſhall riſe

" The flow'ry Shrub of thouſand Dies :

" Yon Wall that feels the ſouthern Ray,

" Shall bluſh with ruddy Fruitage gay :

" While thick beneath its Aſpeƈt warm

" O'er well rang'd Hives the Bees ſhall ſwarm,

" From which, e'er long, of golden Gleam

" Metheglin's luſcious Juice ſhall ſtream :

" This awkward Hutt, o'er-grown with Ivy,

" We'll alter to a modern Privy :

" Up yon green Slope, of Hazels trim,

" An Avenue ſo cool and dim,

" Shall to an Arbour at the End,

" In ſpite of Gout, intice a Friend.

" My Predeceſſor lov'd Devotion ——

" But of a Garden had no Notion."

Continuing

Continuing this fantaftic Farce on,
He now commences Country Parfon.
To make his Character entire,
He weds—a Coufin of the 'Squire;
Not over weighty in the Purfe,
But many Doctors have done worfe:
And though fhe boafts no Charms divine,
Yet fhe can carve, and make Birch Wine.

Thus fixt, content he taps his Barrel,
Exhorts his Neighbours not to quarrel;
Finds his Church-wardens have Difcerning
Both in good Liquor and good Learning;
With Tythes his Barns replete he fees,
And chuckles o'er his Surplice-fees;
Studies to find out latent Dues,
And regulates the *State* of Pews;
Rides a fleek Mare with purple Houfing,
To fhare the monthly Club's caroufing;
Of Oxford Pranks facetious tells,
And—but on Sundays—hears no Bells;
Sends Prefents of his choiceft Fruit,
And prunes himfelf each faplefs Shoot;
Plants Colliflow'rs, and boafts to rear
The earlieft Melon of the Year;

C

Thinks Alteration charming Work is,
Keeps Bantam Cocks, and feeds his Turkies;
Builds in his Copfe a favourite Bench,
And ftores the Pond with Carp and Tench:—

But ah! too foon his thoughtlefs Breaft.
By Cares domeftic is oppreft;
And a third Butcher's Bill, and Brewing,
Threaten inevitable Ruin:
For Children frefh Expences yet,
And *Dicky* now for School is fit.
" Why did I fell my College Life
" (He cries) for Benefice and Wife?
" Return, ye Days! when endlefs Pleafure
" I found in Reading, or in Leifure!
" When calm around the Common Room
" I puff'd my daily. Pipe's Perfume!
" Rode for a Stomach, and infpected,
" At annual Bottlings, Corks felected:
" And din'd untax'd, untroubled, under
" The Portrait of our pious Founder!
" When *Impofitions* were fupply'd
" To light my Pipe——or footh my Pride!
" No Cares were then for forward Peas
" A yearly-longing Wife to pleafe;

" My

" My Thoughts no Chrift'ning Dinners croft,
" No Children cry'd for butter'd Toaft;
" And every Night I went to Bed,
" Without a *Modus* in my Head!"

Oh! trifling Head, and fickle Heart!
Chagrin'd at whatfoe'er thou art;
A Dupe to Follies yet untry'd,
And fick of Pleafures fcarce enjoy'd!
Each Prize poffefs'd, thy Tranfport ceafes,
And in Purfuit alone it pleafes.

A N

EVENING CONTEMPLATION

In a COLLEGE.

Being a PARODY *on* GRAY's ELEGY *in a*
COUNTRY CHURCH-YARD.

THE Curfew tolls the Hour of clofing Gates,
    With jarring Sound the Porter turns the Key,
Then in his dreary Manfion flumb'ring waits,
And flowly, fternly quits it —— tho' for me.

Now

Now fhine the Spires beneath the paly Moon,
And through the Cloifter Peace and Silence reign,
Save where fome Fiddler fcrapes a drowfy Tune,
Or copious Bowls infpire a jovial Strain :

Save that in yonder Cobweb-mantled Room,
Where lies a Student in profound Repofe,
Opprefs'd with Ale, wide-echoes thro' the Gloom
The droning Mufic of his vocal Nofe.

Within thofe Walls, where thro' the glimm'ring Shade
Appear the Pamphlets in a mould'ring Heap,
Each in his narrow Bed till Morning laid,
The peaceful Fellows of the College fleep.

The tinkling Bell proclaiming early Pray'rs,
The noify Servants rattling o'er their Head,
The Calls of Bufinefs, and domeftic Cares,
Ne'er rouze thefe Sleepers from their downy Bed.

No chatt'ring Females crowd their focial Fire,
No Dread have they of Difcord and of Strife ;
Unknown the Names of Hufband and of Sire,
Unfelt the Plagues of matrimonial Life.

Oft have they bafk'd along the funny Walls,
Oft have the Benches bow'd beneath their Weight :
How jocund are their Looks when Dinner calls !
How fmoke the Cutlets on their crowded Plate !

O let

O let not Temp'rance too-difdainful hear
How long our Feafts, how long our Dinners laft :
Nor let the Fair with a contemptuous Sneer
On thefe unmarry'd Men Reflections caft !

The fplendid Fortune and the beauteous Face
(Themfelves confefs it, and their Sires bemoan)
Too foon are caught by Scarlet and by Lace :
Thefe Sons of Science fhine in Black alone.

Forgive, ye Fair, th' involuntary Fault,
If thefe no Feats of Gaiety difplay,
Where through proud Ranelaugh's wide-echoing Vault
Melodious *Frafi* trills her quav'ring Lay.

Say, is the Sword well fuited to the Band,
Does broider'd Coat agree with fable Gown,
Can Drefden Laces fhade a Churchman's Hand,
Or Learning's Vot'ries ape the Beaux of Town?

Perhaps in thefe Time-tott'ring Walls refide
Some who were once the Darlings of the Fair ;
Some who of old could Taftes and Fafhions guide,
Controul the Manager and awe the Play'r.

But Science now has fill'd their vacant Mind
With Rome's rich Spoils and Truth's exalted Views ;
Fir'd them with Tranfports of a nobler Kind,
And bade them flight all Females——but the Mufe.

Full many a Lark, high-tow'ring to the Sky,
Unheard, unheeded, greets th' Approach of Light;
Full many a Star, unseen by mortal Eye,
With twinkling Lustre glimmers thro' the Night.

Some future *Herring*, that with dauntless Breast
Rebellion's Torrent shall like him oppose;
Some mute, some thoughtless *Hardwicke* here may rest,
Some *Pelham*, dreadful to his Country's Foes.

From Prince and People to command Applause,
'Midst ermin'd Peers to guide the high Debate,
To shield Britannia's and Religion's Laws,
And steer with steady Course the Helm of State,

Fate yet forbids; nor circumscribes alone
Their growing Virtues, but their Crimes confines;
Forbids in Freedom's Veil t' insult the Throne,
Beneath her Mask to hide the worst Designs.

To fill the madding Crowd's perverted Mind
With " Pensions, Taxes, Marriages and Jews ;"
Or shut the Gates of Heav'n on lost Mankind,
And wrest their darling Hopes, their future Views.

Far from the giddy Town's tumultuous Strife,
Their Wishes yet have never learn'd to stray;
Content and happy in a single Life,
They keep the noiseless Tenor of their Way.

E'en

E'en now their Books from Cobwebs to protect,
Inclos'd by Doors of Glafs, in Doric Style,
On fluted Pillars rais'd, with Bronzes deck'd,
They claim the paffing Tribute of a Smile.

Oft are the Author's Names, tho' richly bound,
Mif-fpelt by blund'ring Binders' Want of Care;
And many a Catalogue is ftrow'd around,
To tell th' admiring Gueft what Books are there.

For who, to thoughtlefs Ignorance a Prey,
Neglects to hold fhort Dalliance with a Book;
Who there but wifhes to prolong his Stay,
And on thofe Cafes cafts a ling'ring Look?

Reports attract the Lawyer's parting Eyes,
Novels Lord Fopling and Sir Plume require;
For Songs and Plays the Voice of Beauty cries,
And Senfe and Nature Grandifon defire.

For thee, who mindful of thy lov'd Compeers
Doft in their Lines their artlefs Tales relate,
If chance, with prying Search, in future Years,
Some Antiquarian fhall enquire thy Fate,

Haply fome Friend may fhake his hoary Head,
And fay, ' Each Morn, unchill'd by Frofts, he ran
' With Hofe ungarter'd, o'er yon turfy Bed,
' To reach the Chapel ere the Pfalms began.

' There

‘ There in the Arms of that lethargic Chair,.
‘ Which rears it's moth-devoured Back ſo high,.
‘ At Noon he quaff'd three Glaſſes to the Fair,.
‘ And por'd upon the News with curious Eye.

  ‘ Now by the Fire,. engag'd in ſerious Talk
‘ Or mirthful Converſe, would he loit'ring ſtand ;
‘ Then in the Garden chuſe a ſunny Walk,
‘ Or launch the poliſh'd Bowl with ſteady Hand ;

  ‘ One Morn we miſs'd him at the Hour of Pray'r,.
‘ Beſide the Fire, and on his fav'rite Green ;
‘ Another came, nor yet within the Chair,
‘ Nor yet at Bowls, nor Chapel was he ſeen.

  ‘ The next we heard that in a neighb'ring Shire,
‘ That Day to Church he led a bluſhing Bride ;
‘ A Nymph, whoſe ſnowy Veſt and maiden Fear
‘ Improv'd her Beauty while the Knot was ty'd.

  ‘ Now by his Patron's bounteous Care remov'd,
‘ He roves enraptur'd through the Fields of Kent ;
‘ Yet ever mindful of the Place he lov'd,
‘ Read here the Letter which he lately ſent.’

The LETTER.

“ In rural Innocence ſecure I dwell,
“ Alike to Fortune and to Fame unknown ;
“ Approving Conſcience cheers my humble Cell,
“ And ſocial Quiet marks me for her own.

“ Next

" Next to the Bleſſings of religious Truth,
" Two Gifts my endleſs Gratitude engage ;
" A Wife, the Joy and Tranſport of my Youth,
" Now, with a Son, the Comfort of my Age.

" Seek not to draw me from this kind Retreat,
" In loftier Spheres unfit, untaught to move ;
" Content with calm, domeſtic Life, where meet
" The Smiles of Friendſhip, and the Sweets of Love."

The

The PHAETON,

AND THE

ONE HORSE CHAIR.

AT *Blagrave's* * once upon a Time,
There ſtood a PHAETON ſublime:
Unſullied by the duſty Road
Its Wheels with recent Crimſon glow'd;

* Well known at *Oxford* for letting out Carriages, 1763.

It's

It's Sides difplay'd a dazzling Hue,,
It's Harnefs tight, it's Lining new :
No fcheme-enamour'd Youth, I ween,
Survey'd the gaily deck'd Machine,
But fondly long'd to feize the Reins,
And whirl o'er *Campsfield's* † tempting Plains.
Meantime it chanc'd, that hard at hand
A ONE HORSE CHAIR had took it's Stand ;
When thus our Vehicle begun
To fneer the lucklefs *Chaife and One.*

" How could my Mafter place me here
Within thy vulgar Atmofphere ?
From claffic Ground pray fhift thy Station,
Thou Scorn of *Oxford* Education,
Your homely Make, believe me, Man,
Is quite upon the Gothic Plan ;
And you, and all your clumfy Kind,
For lowest Purpofes defign'd :
Fit only, with a one-ey'd Mare,
To drag, for Benefit of Air,
The country Parfon's pregnant Wife,
Thou Friend of dull *domeftic* Life !
Or, with his Maid and Aunt, to School
To carry *Dicky* on a Stool :

† In the Road to *Blenheim.*

Or,

Or, haply to fome Chriftening gay,
A brace of Godmothers convey.——
Or, when bleft *Saturday* prepares
For *London* Tradefmen Reft from Cares,
'Tis thine to make them happy one Day,
Companion of their genial *Sunday!*
'Tis thine, o'er Turnpikes newly made,
When timely Show'rs the Duft have laid,
To bear fome Alderman ferene
To *fragrant* Hampftead's *fylvan* Scene.
Nor higher fcarce thy Merit rifes
Among the polifh'd Sons of *Ifis.*
Hir'd for a folitary Crown,
Canft thou to *Schemes* invite the *Gown?*
Go, tempt fome Prig, pretending Tafte,
With Hat new cock'd, and newly lac'd,
O'er Mutton-chops, and fcanty Wine,
At humble *Dorchefter* to dine!
Meantime remember, lifelefs Drone!
I carry *Bucks* and *Bloods* alone.
And oh! whene'er the Weather's friendly,
What Inn at *Abingdon* or *Henly,*
But ftill my vaft Importance feels,
And gladly greets my entering Wheels.
And think, obedient to the Thong,
How yon gay Street we fmoak along:

While

While All with envious Wonder view
The Corner turn'd fo *quick* and *true*."

To check an Upftart's empty Pride,
Thus fage the ONE HORSE CHAIR reply'd.

" Pray, when the Confequence is weigh'd,
What's all your Spirit and Parade ?
From Mirth to Grief what fad Tranfitions,
To Broken Bones and *Impofitions !*
Or if no Bones are broke, what's worfe,
Your *Schemes* make Work for *Glafs* * and *Nurfe.*—
On Us pray fpare your keen Reproaches,
From *One Horfe Chairs* Men rife to *Coaches* ;
If calm Difcretion's ftedfaft Hand,
With cautious Skill the Reins command.
From me fair *Health*'s frefh Fountain fprings,
O'er me foft *Snugnefs* fpreads her Wings :
And *Innocence* reflects her Ray
To gild my calm fequefter'd Way :
E'en King's might quit their State to fhare
Contentment and a *One Horfe Chair.*—
What though, o'er yonder echoing Street
Your rapid Wheels refound fo fweet ;
Shall *Ifis'* Sons thus vainly prize
A RATTLE *of a larger Size ?*"

* Eminent Surgeons in *Oxford.*

BLAGRAVE,

BLAGRAVE, who during the Difpute,.
Stood in a Corner, fnug and mute,
Surpriz'd, no Doubt, in lofty Verfe,
To hear his Carriages converfe,
With folemn Face, o'er *Oxford* Ale,
To me difclos'd this wonderous Tale :
I ftrait difpatch'd it to the Mufe,
Who brufh'd it up for *Jackfon*'s * News,.
And, what has oft been penn'd in Profe,.
Added this Moral at the Clofe.

" Things may be ufeful if obfcure ;
" The Pace that's flow is often fure :
" When empty Pageantries we prize,.
" We raife but Duft to blind our Eyes..
" The GOLDEN MEAN can beft beftow
" *Safety* for unfubftantial *Show*."

* *Jackfon*'s OXFORD JOURNAL; where this FABLE
firft appeared.

THE

THE

SPLENDID SHILLING.

- - - - - - - - - - - Sing, Heavenly Mufe,
Things unattempted yet, in Profe or Rhime,
A SHILLING, BREECHES, and CHIMERAS dire.

HAPPY the Man, who void of Cares and Strife,
In Silken or in Leathern Purfe, retains
A SPLENDID SHILLING: He nor hears with Pain
New Oyfters cry'd, nor fighs for cheerful Ale;
But with his Friends, when nightly Mifts arife,
To Jun'per's Magpye, or 'Town-hall * repairs:

* Two noted Alehoufes in Oxford, 1700.

Where,

Where mindful of the Nymph, whose wanton Eye
Transfix'd his Soul, and kindled amourous Flames,
CLOE or PHILLIS; he each circling Glass
Wisheth her Health, and Joy, and equal Love.
Mean while, he smokes, and laughs at merry Tale,
Or *Pun* ambiguous, or *Conundrum* quaint.
But I, whom griping Penury surrounds,
And Hunger, sure Attendant upon Want,
With scanty Offals, and small acid Tiff,
(Wretched Repast!) my meagre Corpse sustain:
Then solitary walk, or doze at home
In Garret vile, and with a warming Puff
Regale chill'd Fingers; or from Tube as black
As Winter-Chimney, or well-polish'd Jet,
Exhale *Mundungus*, ill-perfuming Scent:
Not blacker Tube, nor of a shorter Size
Smokes *Cambro-Briton* (vers'd in Pedigree,
Sprung from *Cadwaladur* and *Arthur*, Kings
Full famous in romantic Tale) when he
O'er many a craggy Hill and barren Cliff,
Upon a Cargo of fam'd *Cestrian* Cheese,
High over-shadowing, rides, with a Design
To vend his Wares, or at the *Arvovian* Mart,
Or *Maridunum*, or the antient Town
Yclep'd *Brechinia*, or where *Vaga*'s Stream
Encircles *Aricenium*, fruitful Soil!

Whence

Whence flow nectareous Wines, that well may vie
With *Maſſic*, *Setin*, or renown'd *Falern*.

Thus, while my joyleſs Minutes tedious flow,
With Looks demure, and ſilent Pace, a *Dun*,
Horrible Monſter! hated by Gods and Men,
To my aërial Citadel aſcends;
With vocal Heel thrice thund'ring at my Gate,
With hideous Accent thrice he calls; I know
The Voice ill-boding, and the ſolemn Sound.
What ſhou'd I do? or whither turn? Amaz'd,
Confounded, to the dark Receſs I fly
Of Woodhole; ſtrait my briſtling Hairs erect
Through ſudden Fear; a chilly Sweat bedews
My ſhudd'ring Limbs, and (wonderful to tell!)
My Tongue forgets her Faculty of Speech;
So horrible he ſeems! his faded Brow
Entrench'd with many a Frown, and conic Beard,
And ſpreading Band, admir'd by modern Saints,
Diſaſtrous Acts forebode; in his Right Hand
Long Scrolls of Paper ſolemnly he waves,
With Characters, and Figures dire inſcrib'd,
Grievous to mortal Eyes; (ye Gods avert
Such Plagues from righteous Men;) behind him ſtalks
Another Monſter not unlike himſelf,
Sullen of Aſpect, by the Vulgar call'd

                                        A *Catchpole*,

A *Catchpole*, whose polluted Hands the Gods
With Force incredible, and magick Charms
Erst have endu'd; if he his ample Palm
Should haply on ill-fated Shoulder lay
Of Debtor, strait his Body, to the Touch
Obsequious, (as whilom Knights were wont)
To some inchanted Castle is convey'd,
Where Gates impregnable, and coercive Chains
In Durance strict detain him, till in Form
Of Money, PALLAS sets the Captive free.

    Beware, ye Debtors, when ye walk, beware,
Be circumspect; oft with insidious Ken
This Caitiff eyes your Steps aloof, and oft
Lies perdue in a Nook or gloomy Cave,
Prompt to inchant some inadvertent Wretch
With his unhallowed Touch.   So (Poets sing)
Grimalkin to domestick Vermin sworn
An everlasting Foe, with watchful Eye
Lies nightly brooding o'er a chinky Gap,
Portending her fell Claws, to thoughtless Mice
Sure Ruin.   So her disembowell'd Webb
Arachne in a Hall, or Kitchen spreads,
Obvious to vagrant Flies: She secret stands
Within her woven Cell: The humming Prey,
Regardless of their Fate, rush on the Toils

                Inextricable

Inextricable, nor will aught avail
Their Arts, or Arms, or Shapes of lovely Hue;
The Wafp infidious, and the buzzing Drone,
And Butterfly proud of expanded Wings
Diftinct with Gold, entangled in her Snares,
Ufelefs Refiftance make : With eager Strides,
She tow'ring flies to her expected Spoils ;
Then, with envenom'd Jaws the vital Blood
Drinks of reluctant Foes, and to her Cave
Their bulky Carcaffes triumphant drags.

So pafs my Days.   But when nocturnal Shades
This World invelop, and th' inclement Air
Perfuades Men to repel benumbing Frofts
With pleafant Wines, and crackling Blaze of Wood;
Me, lonely fitting, nor the glimmering Light
Of make-weight Candle, nor the joyous Talk
Of loving Friend delights; diftrefs'd, forlorn,
Amidft the Horrors of the tedious Night,
Darkling I figh, and feed with difmal Thoughts
My anxious Mind; or fometimes mournful Verfe
Indite, and fing of Groves and Myrtle Shades,
Or defperate Lady near a purling Stream,
Or Lover pendent on a Willow Tree.
Mean while I labour with eternal Drought,
And reftlefs wifh, and rave ; my parched Throat

Finds no Relief, nor heavy Eyes Repofe:
But if a Slumber haply does invade
My weary Limbs, my Fancy's ftill awake,
Thoughtful of Drink, and eager, in a Dream,
Tipples imaginary Pots of Ale,
In vain ; awake I find the fettled Thirft
Still gnawing, and the pleafing Fantom curfe.

 Thus do I live, from Pleafure quite debar'd,
Nor tafte the Fruits that the Sun's genial Rays
Mature, *John-Apple*, nor the downy *Peach*;
Nor *Walnut* in rough-furrow'd Coat fecure,
Nor *Medlar-*Fruit, delicious in Decay :
Affliction great! yet greater ftill remain :
My *Galligafkins* that have long withftood
The Winter's Fury, and incroaching Frofts,
By Time fubdu'd, (what will not Time fubdue!)
An horrid Chafm difclofe, with Orifice
Wide, difcontinuous ; at which the Winds
Eurus and *Aufter*, and the dreadful Force
Of *Boreas*, that congeals the *Cronian* Waves,
Tumultuous enter with dire chilling Blafts,
Portending Agues. Thus a well-fraught Ship
Long fail'd fecure, or thro' th' *Ægean* Deep,
Or the *Ionian*, 'till cruizing near
The *Lilybean* Shore, with hideous Crufh

On

On *Scylla*, or *Charybdis* (dang'rous Rocks!)
She ftrikes rebounding, whence the fhatter'd Oak,
So fierce a Shock unable to withftand,
Admits the Sea; in at the gaping Side
The crowding Waves gufh with impetuous Rage,
Refiftlefs, overwhelming; Horrors feize
The Mariners, Death in their Eyes appears,
They ftare, they lave, they pump, they fwear, they pray:
(Vain Efforts!) ftill the battering Waves rufh in,
Implacable, till delug'd by the Foam,
'The Ship finks found'ring in the vaft Abyfs.

A Panegyric on OXFORD ALE.

BY A GENTLEMAN OF OXFORD.

- - - - - - - - Mea nec Falernæ
Temperant vites, neque Formiani
                 Pocula Colles.   HOR.

B ALM of my Cares, sweet Solace of my Toils,
    Hail JUICE benignant! O'er the costly Cups
Of Riot-stirring Wine, unwholesome Draught,
Let Pride's loose Sons prolong the wasteful Night;

My fober Ev'ning let the Tankard blefs,
With Toaft embrown'd, and fragrant Nutmeg fraught,
While the rich Draught with oft-repeated Whiffs
Tobacco mild improves. Divine repaft!
Where no crude Surfeit, or intemperate Joys
Of lawlefs Bacchus reign; but o'er my Soul
A calm Lethean creeps; in drowfy Trance
Each Thought fubfides, and fweet Oblivion wraps
My peaceful Brain, as if the leaden Rod
Of magic Morpheus o'er mine Eyes had fhed
Its opiate Influence. What tho' fore Ills
Opprefs, dire Want of chill-difpelling Coals
Or cheerful Candle (fave the Make-weight's Gleam
Haply remaining) heart-rejoicing ALE
Cheers the fad Scene, and every Want fupplies.

    Meantime, not mindlefs of the daily Tafk
Of Tutor fage, upon the learned Leaves
Of deep SMIGLECIUS much I meditate;
While ALE infpires, and lends its kindred Aid,
The thought-perplexing Labour to purfue,
Sweet Helicon of Logic! But if Friends
Cogenial call me from the toilfome Page,
To Pot-houfe I repair, the facred Haunt,
Where, ALE, thy Votaries in full Refort,
Hold Rites nocturnal. In capacious Chair
Of monumental Oak and antique Mould,

                                        That

That long has ftood the Rage of conquering Years
Inviolate, (nor in more ample Chair
Smoaks rofy Juftice, when th' important Caufe,
Whether of Hen-rooft, or of mirthful Rape,
In all the Majefty of Paunch he tries)
Studious of Eafe, and provident, I place
My gladfome Limbs; while in repeated Round
Returns replenifh'd the fucceffive Cup,
And the brifk Fire confpires to genial Joy:
While haply, to relieve the ling'ring Hours
In innocent Delight, amufive Putt
On fmooth Joint-ftool in emblematic Play
The vain Viciffitudes of Fortune fhews.
Nor Reckoning, Name tremendous, me difturbs,
Nor, call'd for, chills my Breaft with fudden Fear;
While on the wonted Door, expreffive Mark,
The frequent Penny ftands defcrib'd to View,
In fnowy Characters and graceful Row.——

    Hail, TICKING! fureft Guardian of Diftrefs!
Beneath thy Shelter, pennylefs I quaff
The cheerful Cup, nor hear with hopelefs Heart
New Oyfters cry'd:—Tho' much the Poet's Friend,
Ne'er yet attempted in poetic Strain,
Accept this Tribute of poetic Praife!

    Nor Proctor thrice with vocal Heel alarms
Our Joys fecure, nor deigns the lowly Roof

Of

Of Pot-houſe ſnug to viſit: wiſer he
The ſplendid Tavern haunts, or Coffee-houſe
Of JAMES or JUGGINS, were the grateful Breath
Of loath'd Tobacco ne'er diffus'd its Balm;
But the lewd Spendthrift, falſly deem'd polite,.
While ſteams around the fragrant Indian Bowl,
Oft damns the vulgar Sons of humbler ALE:
In vain — the Proctor's Voice arreſts their Joys;
Juſt Fate of wanton Pride and looſe Exceſs!
   Nor leſs by Day delightful is thy Draught,
All-pow'rful ALE! whoſe ſorrow-ſoothing Sweets
Oft I repeat in vacant Afternoon,
When tatter'd Stockings aſk my mending Hand
Not unexperienced; while the tedious Toil
Slides unregarded.   Let the tender Swain
Each Morn regale on nerve-relaxing Tea,
Companion meet of languor-loving Nymph:
Be mine each Morn with eager Appetite
And Hunger undiſſembled, to repair
To friendly Buttery; there on ſmoaking Cruſt
And foaming ALE to banquet unreſtrained,
Material Breakfaſt! Thus in ancient Days
Our Anceſtors robuſt, with liberal Cups
Uſher'd the Morn, unlike the ſqueamiſh Sons
Of modern Times: Nor ever had the Might
Of Britons brave decay'd, had thus they fed,

With

With Britifh ALE improving Britifh Worth.

With ALE irriguous, undifmay'd I hear
The frequent Dun afcend my lofty Dome
Importunate : Whether the plaintive Voice
Of Laundrefs fhrill awake my ftartled Ear ;
Or Barber fpruce with fupple Look intrude ;
Or Taylor with obfequious Bow advance ;
Or Groom invade me with defying Front
And ftern Demeanour, whofe emaciate Steeds
(Whene'er or Phœbus fhone with kindlier Beams,.
Or luckier Chance the borrow'd Boots fupply'd)
Had panted oft beneath my goring Steel.
In vain they plead or threat : All-powerful ALE
Excufes new fupplies, and each defcends
With joylefs Pace, and debt-defpairing Looks :
E'en SPACEY with indignant Brow retires,
Fierceft of Duns ! and conquer'd quits the Field.

Why did the Gods fuch various Bleffings pour
On haplefs Mortals, from their grateful Hands
So foon the fhort-liv'd Bounty to recall ? ——
Thus, while improvident of future Ill,
I quaff the lufcious Tankard uncontroll'd,
And thoughtlefs riot in unlicenc'd Blifs ;
Sudden (dire Fate of all Things excellent !)
Th' unpitying Burfar's crofs-affixing Hand
Blafts all my Joys, and ftops my glad Career.

Nor now the friendly Pot-houfe longer yields
A fure Retreat, when Night o'erfhades the Skies;
Nor Sheppard, barbarous Matron, longer gives
The wonted Truft, and Winter ticks no more.

Thus Adam, exil'd from the beauteous Scenes
Of Eden griev'd, no more in fragrant Bow'r
On Fruits divine to feaft, frefh Shade and Vale
No more to vifit, or vine-mantled Grot;
But, all forlorn, the dreary Wildernefs,
And unrejoicing Solitudes to trace:
Thus too the matchlefs Bard, whofe Lay refounds
The Splendid Shilling's Praife, in nightly Gloom
Of lonefome Garret, pin'd for cheerful Ale;
Whofe Steps in Verfe Miltonic I purfue,
Mean Follower: like him with honeft Love
Of Ale divine infpir'd, and Love of Song.
But long may bounteous Heav'n with watchful Care
Avert his haplefs Lot! Enough for me
That burning with cogenial Flame I dar'd
His guiding Steps at Diftance to purfue,
And fing his favorite Theme in kindred Strains.

ODE

ODE to HORROR.

In the *Allegoric, Descriptive, Alliterative, Epithetical, Fantastic, Hyperbolical,* and *Diabolical* STYLE of our modern ODE-WRITERS, and MONODY-MONGERS.

.... *Ferreus ingruit Horror.* VIRG.

O Goddess of the gloomy Scene,
　　Of shadowy Shapes thou black-brow'd Queen;
Thy Tresses dark with Ivy crown'd,
On yonder mould'ring Abby found;
Oft wont from Charnels damp and dim,
To call the sheeted Spectre grim,

While

While as his loose Chains loudly clink,
Thou add'st a Length to every Link :
O thou, that lov'st at Eve to seek
The pensive-pacing Pilgrim meek,
And set'st before his shuddering Eyes
Strange Forms, and Fiends of Giant-size,
As wildly works thy wizzard Will,
Till fear-struck Fancy has her Fill :
Dark Pow'r, whose magic Might prevails
O'er Hermit-rocks, and Fairy-vales ;
O Goddess, erst by * Spenser view'd,
What Time th' Enchanter vile embru'd
His Hands in Florimel's pure Heart,
Till loos'd by steel-clad Britomart :
O thou that erst on Fancy's Wing
Didst terror-trembling † Tasso bring,
To Groves where kept damn'd Furies dire
Their blue-tipt Battlements of Fire ;
Thou that thro' many a darksome Pine,
O'er the rugged Rock recline,
Did'st wake the hollow-whisp'ring Breeze
With care-consumed Eloise :
O thou, with whom in cheerless Cell,
The midnight Clock pale Pris'ners tell ;

* Spenser's Fairy Queen, b. 3. canto 12.
† Gierus. Liberat. b. 14.

O haste.

'O hafte thee, mild *Miltonic* Maid,

'From yonder Yew's fequefter'd Shade;

'More bright than all the fabled Nine,

'Teach me to breathe the folemn Line'!

'O bid my well-rang'd Numbers rife,

Pervious to none but *Attic* Eyes;

O give the Strain that Madnefs moves,

Till every ftarting Senfe approves!

    What felt the *Gallic* * Traveller,

When far in *Arab*-defert drear,

He found within the Catacomb,

Alive, the Terrors of a Tomb?

While many a Mummy through the Shade,

In hieroglyphic Stole array'd,

Seem'd to uprear the myftic Head,

And trace the Gloom with ghoftly Tread;

Thou heardft him pour the ftifled Groan,

HORROR! his Soul was all thy own!

    O Mother of the fire-clad Thought,

O hafte thee from thy grave-like Grot!

(What Time the Witch perform'd the Rite)

Sprung from th' Embrace of TASTE and NIGHT!

O Queen! that erft did'ft thinly fpread

The willowy Leaves o'er † ISIS' Head,

* I do not remember that any poetical Ufe has been made of this Story.   † See ISIS, *an Elegy.*

And to her meek Mien did'ſt diſpenſe
Woe's moſt awful Negligence;
What Time, in Cave, with Viſage pale,
She told her elegiac Tale:
O thou! whom wand'ring WARTON ſaw,
Amaz'd with more than youthful Awe,
As by the pale Moon's glimm'ring Gleam
He mus'd his *melancholy* Theme *:
O curfeu-loving Goddeſs haſte!
O waft me to ſome SCYTHIAN Waſte;
Where, in *Gothic* Solitude,
'Mid Proſpeéts moſt ſublimely rude,
Beneath a rough Rock's gloomy Chaſm,
Thy Siſter ſits, ENTHUSIASM:
Let me with her, in magic Trance,
Hold moſt delirious Dalliance;
Till I, thy penſive Votary,
HORROR, look madly wild like thee;
Until I gain true Tranſport's Shore,
And Life's retiring Scene is o'er;
Aſpire to ſome more azure Sky,
Remote from dim Mortality;
At Length, recline the fainting Head,
In *Druid*-dreams diſſolv'd and dead.

* See *The* PLEASURES *of* MELANCHOLY, *a Poem.*

FREEMAN's
BEST VIRGINIA.

A PIPE of TOBACCO.

In Imitation of

Six Several AUTHORS.

By HAWKINS BROWNE, Efq;

I. A NEW YEAR's ODE.

In Imitation of COLLEY CIBBER.

RECITATIVO.

OLD Battle-array, big with Horror is fled,
And olive-rob'd Peace again lifts up her Head.
Sing, ye Mufes, TOBACCO, the Bleffing of Peace;
Was ever a Nation fo bleffed as this?

F.   A I R.

A I R.

When Summer Suns grow red with Heat,
Tobacco tempers Phoebus' Ire,
When wintry Storms around us beat,
Tobacco chears with gentle Fire.
Yellow Autumn, youthful Spring,
In thy Praises jointly sing.

RECITATIVO.

Like Neptune, Cæsar guards Virginian Fleets,
Fraught with Tobacco's balmy Sweets;
Old Ocean trembles at Britannia's Pow'r,
And Boreas is afraid to roar.

A I R.

Happy Mortal! he who knows
Pleasure which a Pipe bestows;
Curling Eddies climb the Room,
Wafting round a mild Perfume.

RECITATIVO.

Let foreign Climes the Vine and Orange boast,
While Wastes of War deform the teeming Coast,
Britannia, distant from each hostile Sound,
Enjoys a Pipe, with Ease and Freedom crown'd;
E'en restless Faction finds itself most free,
Or if a Slave, a Slave to Liberty.

A I R.

A I R.

Smiling Years that gayly run,
Round the Zodiack with the Sun,
Tell, if ever you have feen
Realms fo quiet and ferene.
BRITISH Sons no longer now
Hurl the Bar, or twang the Bow,
Nor of crimfon Combat think,
But fecurely fmoke and drink.

C H O R U S.

Smiling Years, that gayly run
Round the Zodiack with the Sun,
Tell, if ever you have feen
Realms fo quiet and ferene.

II. Imitation of Mr. A. PHILLIPS.

LITTLE Tube of mighty Pow'r,
　　Charmer of an idle Hour,
Object of my warm Defire,
Lip of Wax, and Eye of Fire:
And thy fnowy taper Waift,
With my Finger gently brac'd;
And thy pretty fwelling Creft,
With my little Stopper preft,

　　　　　　　　　And

And the fweeteft Blifs of Bliffes,
Breathing from thy balmy Kiffes.
Happy thrice, and thrice agen,
Happieft he of happy Men ;
Who when agen the Night returns,.
When agen the Taper burns ;
When agen the Cricket's gay,.
(Little Cricket, full of Play)
Can afford his Tube to feed
With the fragrant INDIAN Weed :
Pleafure for a Nofe divine,
Incenfe of the God of Wine.
Happy thrice, and thrice agen,
Happieft he of happy Men.

III.   Imitation of Mr. THOMPSON.

O Thou, matur'd by glad Hefperian Suns,
   TOBACCO, Fountain pure of limpid Truth,
That looks the very Soul ; whence pouring Thought
Swarms all the Mind ; abforpt is yellow Care,
And at each Puff Imagination burns :
Flafh on thy Bard, and with exalting Fires
Touch the myfterious Lip that chaunts thy Praife,
In Strains to mortal Sons of Earth unknown.
Behold an Engine, wrought from tawny Mines

Of

Of ductile Clay, with plastick Virtue form'd,
And glaz'd magnifick o'er, I grasp, I fill.
From PÆTOTHEKE with pungent Pow'rs perfum'd,
Itself one Tortoise all, where shines imbib'd
Each parent Ray; then rudely ram'd illume
With the red Touch of zeal-enkindling Sheet,
Mark'd with Gibsonian Lore; forth issue Clouds,
Thought-thrilling, thirst-inciting Clouds around,
And many-mining Fires: I all the while,
Lolling at Ease, inhale the breezy Balm.
But chief, when Bacchus wont with thee to join,
In genial Strife and orthodoxal Ale,
Stream Life and Joy into the Muse's Bowl.
Oh be thou still my great Inspirer, thou
My Muse; oh fan me with thy Zephyr's Boon,
While I, in clouded Tabernacle shrin'd,
Burst forth all Oracle and mystick Song.

IV. Imitation of Dr. YOUNG.

CRITICKS avaunt; TOBACCO is my Theme;
Tremble like Hornets at the blasting Steam.
And you, Court-insects, flutter not too near
It's Light, nor buz within the scorching Sphere.
POLLIO, with Flame like thine, my Verse inspire,
So shall the Muse from Smoke elicit Fire.

Coxcombs

Coxcombs prefer the tickling Sting of Snuff;
Yet all their Claim to Wifdom is — a Puff:
Lord FOPLIN fmokes not — for his Teeth afraid:
Sir TAWDRY fmokes not — for he wears Brocade.
Ladies, when Pipes are brought, affect to fwoon;
They love no Smoke, except the Smoke of Town;
But Courtiers hate the puffing Tribe,— no Matter,
Strange if they love the Breath that cannot flatter!
Its Foes but fhew their Ignorance; can he
Who fcorns the Leaf of Knowledge love the Tree?
The tainted Templar (more prodigious yet)
Rails at TOBACCO, though it makes him — fpit.
CITRONIA vows it has an odious Stink;
She will not fmoke (ye Gods!) but fhe will drink:
And chafte PRUDELLA (blame her if you can)
Says, Pipes are us'd by that vile Creature Man:
Yet Crouds remain, who ftill its Worth proclaim,
While fome for Pleafure fmoke, and fome for Fame:
Fame, of our Actions univerfal Spring,
For which we drink, eat, fleep, fmoke,— ev'ry Thing.

V. Imitation of Mr. POPE.

BLEST Leaf! whofe aromatick Gales difpenfe
To Templars Modefty, to Parfons Senfe:
So raptur'd Priefts, at fam'd DODONA's Shrine:
Drank Infpiration from the Steam divine.

Poifon

Poifon that cures, a Vapour that affords
Content, more folid than the Smile of Lords:
Reft to the Weary, to the Hungry Food,
The laft kind Refuge of the Wife and Good.
Infpir'd by thee, dull Cits adjuft the Scale
Of Europe's Peace, when other Statefmen fail.
By thee protected, and thy Sifter, Beer,
Poets rejoice, nor think the Bailiff near.
Nor lefs the Critick owns thy genial Aid,
While fupperlefs he plies the piddling Trade.
What though to Love and foft Delights a Foe,
By Ladies hated, hated by the Beau,
Yet focial Freedom, long to Courts unknown,
Fair Health, fair Truth, and Virtue are thy own.
Come to thy Poet, come with healing Wings,
And let me tafte thee unexcis'd by Kings.

VI. Imitation of DEAN SWIFT.

BOY! bring an Ounce of FREEMAN's beft,
 And bid the Vicar be my Gueft:
Let all be plac'd in Manner due,
A Pot wherein to fpit or fpue,
And London Journal, and Free-Briton,
Of ufe to light a Pipe, or * * * * *
* * * * * * * * * * * * * * * * * * *
* * * * * * * * * * * * * * * *

    This

This Village, unmolefted yet,
By Troopers, fhall be my Retreat :
Who cannot flatter, bribe, betray ;
Who cannot write or vote for Pay.
Far from the Vermin of the Town,
Here let me rather live, my own,
Doze o'er a Pipe, whofe Vapour bland
In fweet Oblivion lulls the Land,
Of all which at Vienna paffes,
As ignorant as * * * Brafs is :
And fcorning Rafcals to carefs,
Extoll the Days of good Queen BESS,
When firft TOBACCO bleft our Ifle,
Then think of other Queens — and fmile.

   Come jovial Pipe, and bring along
   Midnight Revelry and Song ;
   The merry Catch, the Madrigal,
   That echoes fweet in City Hall ;
   The Parfon's Pun, the fmutty Tale
   Of Country Juftice o'er his Ale.
   I afk not what the French are doing,
   Or Spain to compafs Britain's Ruin :
     Britons, if undone, can go,
     Where TOBACCO loves to grow.

T H E

PLEASURE *of being* OUT OF DEBT.

HORACE, Ode XXII. Book 1. imitated.

Integer vitæ fcelerifque purus, &c.

I.

THE Man, who not a Farthing owes,
    Looks down with fcornful Eye on thofe,
    Who rife by Fraud and Cunning;
Though in the *Pig-market* he ftand
With Afpect grave and clear-ftarch'd Band,
    He fears no Tradefman's Dunning.

H. He

II.

He paffes by each Shop in Town,
Nor hides his Face beneath his Gown,
    No Dread his Heart invading ;
He quaffs the Nectar of the *Tuns*,
Or on a fpur-gall'd Hackney runs
    To London mafquerading.

III.

What Joy attends a new-paid Debt !
Our Manciple I lately met
    Of Vifage wife and prudent ;
I on the Nail by Battels paid,
The Monfter turn'd away difmay'd,
    Hear this, each *Oxford* Student !

IV.

With Juftice and with Truth to trace
The griefly Features of his Face,
    Exceeds all Man's recounting ;
Suffice, he look'd as grim and four
As any Lion in the Tower,
    Or half-ftarv'd Cat-a-Mountain.

V.

A Phiz fo grim you fcarce can meet
In Bedlam, Newgate, or the Fleet,
    Dry Nurfe of Faces horrid !

Not

Not BUCKHORSE fierce, with many a Bruife;
Difplays fuch complicated Hues
   On his undaunted Forehead.

VI.

Place me on Scotland's bleakeft Hill,
Provided I can pay my Bill,.
   Hang ev'ry Thought of Sorrow;
There falling Sleet, or Froft, or Rain,.
Attack a Soul refolv'd, in vain : - - - -
   It may be fair To-morrow..

VII.

To *Heddington* then let me ftray,
And take *Joe Pullen's Tree* away,
   I'll ne'er complain of Phœbus ;
But while he fcorches up the Grafs,
I'll fill a Bumper to my Lafs,
   And toaft her in a Rebus.

ODE TO AN EAGLE,

Confined in a COLLEGE COURT.

Quis tam crudeles optavit sumere pænas,
Cui tantum de te licuit ? - - - - -   VIRG.

Atque affigit humi divinæ particulam auræ. HOR.

I.

I Mperial Bird, who wont to soar
   High o'er the rolling Cloud,
Where Hyperborean Mountains hoar
   Their Heads in Ether shroud; ——

Thou

Thou Servant of almighty Jove,.
Who, free and fwift as Thought, could'ft rove
To the bleak North's extremeft Goal ;———
Thou, who magnanimous could'ft bear
The fovereign Thund'rer's Arms in Air,,
And fhake thy native Pole !———

II..

Oh cruel Fate ! what barbarous Hand,.
What more than Gothic Ire,
At fome fierce Tyrant's dread Command,.
To check thy daring Fire,
Has plac'd thee in this fervile Cell,
Where Difcipline and Dulnefs dwell ;
Where Genius ne'er was feen to roam :.
Where ev'ry felfifh Soul's at reft,
Nor ever quits the carnal Breaft,
But lurks and fneaks at Home !

III.

Though dim'd thine Eye, and clipt thy Wing,
So grov'ling ! once fo great !
The grief-infpired Mufe fhall fing
In tend'reft Lays thy Fate :
What Time by thee fcholaftic Pride,
Takes his precife, pedantic Stride,

No

Nor on thy Mis'ry cafts a Care;
The Stream of Love ne'er from his Heart
Flows out, to act fair Pity's Part;
    But ftinks, and ftagnates there.

IV.

Yet ufeful ftill, hold to the Throng ——
    Hold the reflecting Glafs, ——
That not untutor'd at thy Wrong
    The Paffenger may pafs:
Thou Type of Wit and Senfe confin'd,
Cramp'd by th' Oppreffors of the Mind;
    Born to look downward on the Ground!
Type of the Fall of Greece and Rome!
While more than mathematic Gloom,
    Envelopes all around!

THE

ART OF PREACHING,

A FRAGMENT.

In Imitation of HORACE's ART OF POETRY.

By the late Rev. CHRISTOPHER PITT.

- - - *Pendent opera interrupta.* - - -

SHOULD some fam'd Hand, in this fantastic Age,
   Draw RICH, as RICH appears upon the Stage,
With all his Postures, in one motley Plan,
The God, the Hound, the Monkey, and the Man;

Here

Here o'er his Head high-brandifhing a Leg,
And there juft hatch'd, and breaking from his Egg;
While Monfter crowds on Monfter through the Piece,
Who could help laughing at a Sight like this?
Or as a Drunkard's Dream together brings
A Court of Coblers, and a Mob of Kings;
Such is a Sermon, where confus'dly dark,
Join *Hoadly, Sharp, South, Sherlock, Wake,* and *Clarke.*
So Eggs of different Parifhes will run
To batter, when you beat fix Yolks to one;
So fix bright chymic Liquors if you mix,
In one dark Shadow vanifh all the fix.

This Licence Priefts and Painters ever had,
To run bold Lengths, but never to run mad;
For thefe can't reconcile God's Grace to Sin,
Nor thofe paint Tygers in an Afs's Skin;
No common Dauber in one Piece would join
A Fox and Goofe, - - - unlefs upon a Sign.

Some fteal a Page of Senfe from *Tillotfon,*
And then conclude divinely with their own;
Like Oil on Water mounts the Prelate up,
His Grace is always fure to be at Top;
That Vein of Mercury it's Beams will fpread,
And fhine more ftrongly through a Mine of Lead.
With fuch low Arts your Hearers never bilk,
For who can bear a Fuftian lin'd with Silk?

Sooner

Sooner than preach such Stuff, I'd walk the Town,
Without my Scarf in *Whiston*'s draggled Gown;
Ply at the *Chapter* and at *Child*'s to read
For Pence, and bury for a Groat a Head.

 Some easy Subject chuse, within your Power,
Or you will ne'er hold out for Half an Hour.
Still to your Hearers all your Sermons sort;
Who'd preach against Corruption at the Court?
Against Church Pow'r at Visitations bawl?
Or talk about Damnation at *Whitehall?*
Harangue the Horse-guards on a Cure of Souls?
Condemn the Quirks of Chancery at the *Rolls?*
Or rail at Hoods and Organs at St. *Paul*'s?
Or be, like *David Jones*, so indiscreet,
To rave at Usurers in *Lombard-street?*

 Begin with Care, nor, like that Curate vile,
Set out in this high prancing stumbling Style;
" Whoever with a piercing *Eye* can *see*,
" Through the *past* Records of *Futurity*"—
All gape, no Meaning:—the puft Orator
Talks much, and says just nothing, for an Hour.
Truth and the Text he labours to display,
Till both are quite interpreted away:
So frugal Dames insipid Water pour,
Till Green, Bohea, or Coffee are no more.

His

His Arguments in giddy Circles run
Still round and round, and end where they begun:
So the poor Turnfpit, as the Wheel runs round,
The more he gains, the more he lofes Ground.
Nor Parts diftinct, or general Scheme we find,
But one wild fhapelefs Monfter of the Mind :
So when old Bruin teems, her Children fail
Of Limbs, Form, Figure, Features, Head or Tail;
Nay, though fhe licks the Ruins, all her Cares
Scarce mend the Lumps, and bring them but to Bears.

   Ye Country Vicars, when you preach in Town
A Turn at *Paul's*, to pay your Journey down,
If you would fhun the Sneer of every Prig,
Lay by the little Band, and rufty Wig :
But yet be fure, your proper Language know,
Nor talk as born within the Sound of *Bow*.
Speak not the Phrafe that *Drury-lane* affords,
Nor from *'Change-alley* fteal a Cant of Words.
Coachmen will criticife your Style, nay further,
Porters will bring it in for *Wilful Murder* ;
The Dregs of the Canaille will look afkew
To hear the Language of the Town from you ;
Nay, my Lord May'r, with Merriment poffeft,
Will break his Nap, and laugh among the reft,
And jog the Aldermen to hear the Jeft,

* * * * * * o * * * * * *

THE

CELEBRATED SONG

OF THE

All-Souls MALLARD.

GRIFFIN, Buſtard, Turkey, Capon,
  Let other hungry Mortals gape on ;
And on the Bones their Stomach fall hard,
But let All-Souls Men have their MALLARD.
    Oh ! by the Blood of King Edward,
    Oh ! by the Blood of King Edward,
    It was a ſwapping, ſwapping MALLARD.

F 2   The

The *Romans* once admir'd a *Gander*
More than they did their chief Commander:
Becaufe he fav'd, if fome don't fool us,
The Place that's call'd from th' *Head of Tolus*.
          Oh! by the Blood, &c.

The Poets feign'd *Jove* turn'd a Swan,
But let them prove it, if they can:
As for our Proof 'tis not at all hard,
For it was a fwapping, fwapping MALLARD.
          Oh! by the Blood, &c.

Swapping he was from Bill to Eye;
Swapping he was from Wing to Thigh;
His fwapping Tool of Generation
Out-fwapped all the wing'd Creation:
          Oh! by the Blood, &c.

Therefore let us fing and dance a Galliard,
To the Remembrance of the MALLARD:
And as the MALLARD dives in Pool,
Let us dabble, dive, and duck in Bowl.
       Oh! by the Blood of King Edward,
       Oh! by the Blood of King Edward,
       It was a fwapping, fwapping MALLARD.

SONG,

S O N G,

In Honour of the Celebration of the BOAR's HEAD,

At QUEEN's COLLEGE, OXFORD.

Tam Marti quam Mercurio.

I Sing not of Roman or Grecian mad Games,
   The Pythian, Olympic, and such like hard Names;
Your Patience awhile with Submission I beg,
I strive but to honour the Feast of Coll. Reg.
       Derry down, down, down, derry down.

No Thracian Brawls at our Rites ere prevail,
We temper our Mirth with plain sober mild Ale;
The Tricks of old Circe deter us from Wine;
Though we honour a Boar, we won't make ourselves
    Swine.   Derry down, &c.

                      Great

Great Milo was famous for flaying his Ox,
Yet he prov'd but an Afs in cleaving of Blocks:
But we had a Hero for all Things was fit,
Our Motto difplays both his Valour and Wit.

Derry down, &c.

Stout Hercules labour'd, and look'd mighty big,
When he flew the half-ftarv'd Erymanthian Pig,
But we can relate fuch a Stratagem taken,
That the ftouteft of Boars, could not *fave his own Bacon.*

Derry down, &c.

So dreadful this briftle-back'd Foe did appear,
You'd have fworn he had got the wrong *Pig by the Ear.*
But inftead of avoiding the Mouth of the Beaft,
He ramm'd in a Volume, and cry'd—*Græcum eft.*

Derry down, &c.

In this gallant Action fuch Fortitude fhewn is,
As proves him no Coward, nor tender Adonis;
No Armour but Logic; by which we may find
That Logic's the Bulwark of Body and Mind.

Derry down, &c.

Ye Squires that fear neither Hills nor rough Rocks,
And think you're full wife when you outwit a Fox;
Enrich your poor Brains, and expofe them no more,
Learn Greek, and feek Glory from hunting the Boar.

Derry down, &c.

EPIGRAM *on an* EPIGRAM.

I.

ONE Day in *Chriſt-Church* Meadows walking,
    Of Poetry, and ſuch Things talking,
        Says *Ralph*, a merry Wag,
An EPIGRAM, if right and good,
In all its Circumſtances ſhou'd
        Be like a *Jelly-Bag.*

II.

Your Simile, I own, is new,
But how do'ft make it out, quoth *Hugh* ?
    Quoth *Ralph*, I'll tell thee, Friend ;
Make it at Top both wide and fit
To hold a Budget-full of Wit,
    And point it at the End *.

* *N. B.* This *Epigram* is printed from the original *Manuſcript*, preſerved in the Archives of the Jelly=Bag Society.

A N

EPISTLE *to* *Mr*. ROBERT LOWTH,

In Imitation of HORACE, Book ii. Epist. 19.

By the late Mr. CHRISTOPHER PITT.

'TIS said, dear Sir, no Poets please the Town;
  Who drink mere Water, though from *Helicon*:
For in cold Blood they seldom boldly think:
Their Rhymes are more insipid than their Drink.
Not great *Apollo* could the Train inspire,
'Till generous *Bacchus* help'd to fan the Fire.

Warm'd

Warm'd by two Gods at once, they drink and write;
Rhyme all the Day, and fuddle all the Night.
Homer, fays *Horace*, nods in many a Place,
But hints, he nodded oftner o'er the Glafs.
Infpir'd with Wine old *Ennius* fung and thought,
With the fame Spirit, that his Heroes fought:
And we from *Johnfon's* Tavern-laws divine
That Bard was no great Enemy to Wine.
'Twas from the Bottle *King* deriv'd his Wit,
Drank till he could not talk, and then he writ.
Let no coif'd Serjeant touch the facred Juice,
But leave it to the Bards for better Ufe :
Let the grave Judges too the Glafs forbear,
Who never fing and dance but once a Year.
This Truth once known, our Poets take the Hint,
Get drunk or mad, and then get into Print :
To raife their Flames indulge the mellow Fit,
And lofe their Senfes in the Search of Wit :
And when with Claret fir'd they take the Pen,
Swear they can write, becaufe they drink, like *Ben*.
Such mimick *Swift* or *Prior* to their Coft,
For in the rafh Attempt the Fools are loft.
When once a Genius breaks through common Rules,
He leads an Herd of imitating Fools.
If *Pope*, the Prince of Poets, fick a-bed,
O'er fteaming Coffee bends his aching Head,

The

The Fools in public o'er the fragrant Draught
Incline thofe Heads, that never ach'd or thought.
This muft provoke his Mirth, or his Difdain,
'Cure his Complaint, —— or make him fick again.
I too, like them, the Poet's Path purfue,
And keep great *Flaccus* ever in my View ;
But in a diftant View — yet what I write,
In thefe loofe Sheets, muft never fee the Light ;
Epiftles, Odes, and twenty Trifles more,
Things that are born and die in Half an Hour.
What ! you muft dedicate, fays fneering *Spence*,
This Year fome new Performance to the Prince :
Though Money is your Scorn, no doubt in Time,
You hope to gain fome vacant Stall by Rhyme ;
Like other Poets, were the Truth but known,
You too admire whatever is your own.
Thefe wife Remarks my Modefty confound,
While the Laugh rifes, and the Mirth goes round ;
Vex'd at the Jeft, yet glad to fhun a Fray,
I whifk into my Coach, and drive away.

THE

L·O W N G E R.

I Rife about nine, get to Breakfaft by ten,
  Blow a Tune on my Flute, or perhaps make a Pen ;
Read a Play 'till eleven, or cock my lac'd Hat ;
Then ftep to my Neighbour's, till Dinner, to chat.
Dinner over, to *Tom*'s, or to *James*'s I go,
The News of the Town fo impatient to know ;
While *Law*, *Locke*, and *Newton*, and all the rum Race,
That talk of their Modes, their Ellipfes, and Space,
The Seat of the Soul, and new Syftems on high,
In Holes, as abftrufe as their Myfteries, lye.

From

From the Coffee-houſe then I to Tennis away,
And at five I poſt back to my College to pray:
I ſup before eight, and ſecure from all Duns,
Undauntedly march to the *Mitre* or *Tuns*;
Where in Punch or good Claret my Sorrows I drown,
And toſs off a Bowl " To the beſt in the Town :"
At One in the Morning, I call what's to pay,
Then Home to my College I ſtagger away,
Thus I tope all the Night, as I trifle all Day.

EPIGRAM, *written by an* EXCISEMAN,

And addreſſed to a young Lady, who was courted at
the ſame Time by an APOTHECARY.

WHAT though the Doctor boaſts to fit
Your *Mortar* to his *Peſtle*;
Are not my *Inches* every whit
As good to *gage* your *Veſſel?*

ON

AN

EPISTLE *to Mr.* SPENCE,

When Tutor to Lord MIDDLESEX.

In Imitation of HORACE, Book i. Epift. 18.

By the late Mr. CHRISTOPHER PITT.

SPENCE, with a Friend you pafs the Hours away
In pointed Jokes, yet innocently gay :
You ever differ'd from a Flatterer more,
Than a chafte Lady from a flaunting Whore.

'Tis

'Tis true you rallied every Fault you found,
But gently tickled, while you cur'd the Wound:
Unlike the paultry Poets of the Town,
Rogues who expose themselves for Half a Crown;
And still impose on ev'ry Soul they meet
Rudeness for Sense, and Ribaldry for Wit:
Who, tho' half-starv'd, in spite of Time and Place,
Repeat their Rhymes, tho' Dinner stays for Grace:
And as their Poverty their Dresses fit,
They think of course a Sloven is a Wit:
But Sense (a Truth these Coxcombs ne'er suspect)
Lies just 'twixt Affectation and Neglect.

One Step, still lower, if you condescend,
To the mean Wretch, the great Man's humble Friend,
That moving Shade, that Pendant at his Ear,
That two-legg'd Dog, still pawing on the Peer.
Studying his Looks, and watching at the Board,
He gapes to catch the Droppings of my Lord;
And tickled to the Soul at ev'ry Joke,
Like a press'd Watch, repeats what t'other spoke:
Echo to Nonsense! such a Scene to hear!
'Tis just like *Punch* and his Interpreter.

On Trifles some are earnestly absurd,
You'll think the World depends on ev'ry Word. —

What

What, is not ev'ry Mortal free to speak ?
I'll give my Reasons, tho' I break my Neck —
And what's the Question ? — if it shines or rains,
Whether 'tis twelve or fifteen Miles to *Staines*.

The Wretch reduc'd to Rags by ev'ry Vice,.
Pride, Projects, Races, Mistresses, and Dice,
The rich Rogue shuns, tho' full as bad as he,.
And knows a Quarrel is good Husbandry.

'Tis strange, cries Peter, you are out of Pelf,.
I'm sure I thought you wiser than myself;.
Yet gives him nothing — but Advice too late,
Retrench, or rather mortgage your Estate,
I can advance the Sum, — 'tis best for both, —
But henceforth cut your Coat to match your Cloth.

A Minister, in mere Revenge and Sport,
Shall give his Foe a paultry Place at Court.
The Dupe for ev'ry royal Birth-day buys
New Horses, Coaches, Cloaths, and Liveries ;
Plies at the Levee, and distinguish'd there
Lives on the Royal Whisper for a Year ;
His Wenches shine in Brussels and Brocade ;
And now the Wretch, ridiculously mad,
Draws on his Banker, mortgages and fails,
Then to the Country runs away from Jails :

There

There ruin'd by the Court he sells a Vote
To the next Burgess, as of old he bought;
Rubs down the Steeds which once his Chariot bore,
Or sweeps the Town which once he *serv'd* before.

But, by this roving Meteor led, I tend
Beyond my Theme, forgetful of my Friend.
Then take Advice; I preach not out of Time,
When good Lord Middlesex is bent on Rhyme.

Their Humour check'd, or Inclination crost,
Sometimes the Friendship of the Great is lost.
Unless call'd out to wench, be sure comply,
Hunt when he hunts, and lay the Fathers by:
For your Reward you gain his Love, and dine
On the best Ven'son and the best French Wine:
Nor to Lord ****** make the Observation,
How the twelve Peers have answer'd their Creation,
Nor in your Wine or Wrath betray your Trust,
Be silent still, and obstinately just:
Explore no Secrets, draw no Characters,
For Echo will repeat, and Walls have Ears:
Nor let a busy Fool a Secret know,
A Secret gripes him till he lets it go:
Words are like Bullets, and we wish in vain,
When once discharg'd, to call them back again.

G   **** Defend,

* * * * * * * * * * * * * * * *

* * * * * * * * * * * * * *

Defend, dear *Spence*, the honeſt and thc civil,
But to cry up a Raſcal ―― that's the Devil.
Who guards a good Man's Charaĉter, 'tis known,
At the ſame Time proteĉts and guards his own.
For as with Houſes, 'tis with People's Names,
A Shed may ſet a Palace all on Flames ;·
The Fire negleĉted on the Cottage preys,
But mounts at laſt into a general Blaze.

'Tis a fine Thing, ſome think, a Lord to know ;
I wiſh his Tradeſmen could but think ſo too.
He gives his Word ―― then all your Hopes are gone :
He gives his Honour ―― then you're quite undone.
His and ſome Women's Love the ſame are found,
You raſhly board a Fireſhip and are drown'd.

Moſt Folks ſo partial to themſelves are grown,
They hate a Temper diff'ring from their own.
The grave abhor the gay, the gay the ſad,
And Formaliſts pronounce the witty mad :
The Sot, who drinks ſix Bottles in a Place,
·Swears at the Flinchers who refuſe their Glaſs.
Would you not paſs for an ill-natur'd Man,
Comply with ev'ry Humour that you can.

Pope

Pope will inftruct you how to pafs away
Your Time like him, and never lofe a Day;
From Hopes or Fears your Quiet to defend,
To all Mankind as to yourfelf a Friend,
And facred from the World, retir'd, unknown,
To lead a Life with Morals like his own.

When to delicious *Pimperne* I retire,
What greater Blifs, my *Spence*, can I defire?
Contented there my eafy Hours I fpend
With Maps, Globes, Books, my Bottle and a Friend.
There can I live upon my Income ftill,
E'en though the Houfe fhould pafs the Quakers Bill:
Yet to my Share fhould fome good Prebend fall,
I think myfelf of Size to fill a Stall.
For Life or Wealth let Heav'n my Lot affign,
A firm and even Soul fhall ftill be mine.

MORNING.

MORNING. *An* ODE.

The Author confined to College.

Scribimus inclufi. - - - - -   PERS. Sat. I. V. 13.

ONCE more the vernal Sun's ambrofial Beams
The Fields, as with a purple Robe adorn:
Charwell, thy fedgy Banks, and glift'ring Streams
‘ All laugh and fing at mild Approach of Morn;
Thro' the deep Groves I hear the chaunting Birds,
And thro' the clóver'd Vale the various-lowing Herds.

Up mounts the Mower from his lowly Thatch,
Well pleas'd the Progrefs of the Spring to mark,
The fragrant Breath of Breezes pure to catch,
And ftartle from her Couch the early Lark;
More genuine Pleafure fooths his tranquil Breaft,
Than high-thron'd Kings can boaft, in eaftern Glory dreft.

The penfive Poet through the Green-wood fteals
Or treads the willow'd Marge of murm'ring Brook;
Or climbs the fteep Afcent of airy Hills;
'There fits him down beneath a branching Oak,
Whence various Scenes, and Profpeĉts wide below,
Still teach his mufing Mind with Fancies high to glow.

But

But I nor with the Day awake to Blifs,
    (Inelegant to me fair Nature's Face,
A Blank the Beauty of the Morning is,
    And Grief and Darknefs all for Light and Grace ;)
Nor bright the Sun, nor green the Meads appear,
Nor Colour charms mine Eye, nor Melody mine Ear.

Me, void of Elegance and Manners mild,
    With leaden Rod, ftern Difcipline reftrains;
Stiff Pedantry, of learned Pride the Child,
    My roving Genius binds in Gothic Chains;
Nor can the cloyfter'd Mufe expand her Wing,
Nor bid thefe twilight Roofs with her gay Carols ring.

On Mifs POLLY FOOTE's

Unexpected Arrival at OXFORD,

And fpeedy Flight from thence, 1758.

LONG had fair *Venus* and her Son
    Diftrefs' *Minerva*'s darling Town
    With Perfecution jealous ;
Of Belles fo fcanty was her Choice,
She fcarce could furnifh Toafts for Boys,
    Or Wives for humbler *Fellows.*

Yet

Yet *Pallas* all their Spleen defy'd,
And prudently the Lofs fupply'd
   Of fuch precarious Bliffes :
Hence were her Sons more ftudious grown :
Her Difcipline went fmoother on,
   'Mid Troops of homely Miffes.

Cupid, who late had feen the Place,
Found they had quite miftook the Cafe,
   That Books would grow in Fafhion,
That dazzling Eyes and blooming Cheeks,
Could only tame thofe hardy *Greeks*,
   And bring them to Submiffion.

Then fwift as Thought he flew to Town,
And *Polly* ftraight is order'd down ;
   The Champion of Beauty ;
For well his Godfhip did devife,
'That *Polly*'s Charms and *Polly*'s Eyes
   Would be alert on Duty.

She came, and with each Grace complete,
From a *Venetian* Window's Height
   Her Battery fhe play'd :
The fatal Slaughter who can tell,
What Troops of gazing Students fell,
   Stretch'd o'er the fmooth *Parade ?*

Sage

Sage Folios, now a mufty Heap,
In Chains and learned Darknefs fleep,
    All Logick's turn'd to Folly;
Each Student takes his Cap and Gown,
And runs through ev'ry Street in Town,
    To catch a Look at *Polly.*

Who now can pedant Rules endure? —
" Go Boy, and bid the beft Frifeur,
    " At Six precife be wi' me;"
My Hair in Wires exaƈt and nice,
I'll trim my Cap to fmalleft Size,
    That *Polly* fure may fee me.

Nay e'en the Don his Pipe foregoes,
That Friend to Wifdom and Repofe,
    Left *Polly* be offended;
And *Galen*'s fageft Sons will leave,
To dangle Hours at *Polly*'s Sleeve,
    Their Patients unattended.

See Churches are forfaken too,
If *Polly* does not grace a Pew,
    To keep grave Heads from fleeping:
Mad *H-tch-nfonians* rave in vain,
The fad deferted Seats remain
    For 'Prentice Boys to weep in.

Cupid,

Cupid, who ſtood at *Polly*'s Side
Incog, and every Shaft ſupplied,
    Laugh'd with inſulting Malice,
To ſee how ſure each Arrow flew,
How at each killing Glance ſhe ſlew
    Some fav'rite Son of *Pallas*.

Then to *Jove*'s Court he wing'd his Way,
To tell the Triumphs of the Day,
    And publiſh *Polly*'s Glory;
But *Pallas* had that Morn been there,
And humbly fought of *Jove* to hear
    The Hardſhips of her Story.

" That all her Sons were Rebels grown,
" No Books were read, no Rules were known;
    " Her fav'rite Seat was undone:"
Her Plea was heard, 'twas *Jove*'s Decree
That *Iris* ſhould next Week convey
    Fair *Polly* back to *London*.

The CUSHION PLOT.

Discovered by Dr. SHAW.

By H. B. Efq;

WHEN *Gaby* Poffeffion had got of the HALL,
He took a Survey of the Chapel and All,
Since that, like the reft, was juft ready to falL
Which nobody can deny.

And firft he began to examine the Cheft,
Where he found an old *Cufhion* which gave him diftafte;
The firft of the Kind that e'er *troubled his Reft.*
Which nobody, &c.

Two Letters of Gold on this Cufhion were rear'd;
Two Letters of Gold once by *Gaby* rever'd,
But now, what was Loyalty, Treafon appear'd:
Which nobody, &c.

" *J. R.* (quoth the Don, in Soliloquy bafs)
" See the Works of this damnable Jacobite Race!
" We'll out with the *J*, and put *G* in it's Place:"
Which nobody, &c.

And now to erafe thefe Letters fo rich,
For Sciffars and Bodkin his Fingers did itch,
For Converts in Politics go *thorough-ftitch.*
Which nobody, &c.

The Thing was almoft as foon done as faid,
Poor *J* was depos'd, and *G* reign'd in his ftead;
Such a quick Revolution fure never was read!
Which nobody, &c.

Then hey for Preferment — But how did he ſtare,
When convinc'd and aſham'd of not being aware,
That *J* ſtood for * JEMMET, for RAYMOND the *R*.

         Which nobody, &c.

Then beware all ye Parents, from hence I adviſe,
How ye chuſe Chriſtian Names for the Babes ye baptize,
For if *Gaby* dont like 'em he'll pick out their *J*'s.

        Which nobody can deny.

On LOPPING New-College LIME TREES.

WHILOM a Row of ſaucy Limes,
  Planted, I ween, in luckleſs Times,
   By ſome ill-favour'd Burſar;
Like Upſtarts vain, grew proud and tall,
And boldly perk'd it o'er the Wall,
   No Trees look'd ever fiercer.

But late for ſundry Crimes arraign'd,
(Whether ſome ſtripling Shrubs complain'd
   Theſe Rogues preſum'd to ſlight 'em,
Or whether they were heard to prate
Of ſome ſad Yew's untimely Fate,
   That once grew over-right 'em:

* The Benefactor who gave the Cuſhion.

            Or

Or if by Chance their Heads they fhook,
When tow'rds the Church they turn'd a Look,
    And mourn'd the fad Conditions
Of poor St. *Peter*'s * num'rous Dead,
That to their Graves were daily led,
    Since fome Folks turn'd Phyficians)

Whate'er the Caufe, fome angry Pow'r
Refolv'd their daring Tops to low'r :
    His murd'rous Mates affembled :
Oh ! as the mangling Crew appears,
Arm'd with Ax, Hatchet, Saw, and Sheers,
    How ev'ry *Dryad* trembled.

Sore Caufe, for ne'er in Grove of Oak
Did fpendthrift Heir's unpity'd Stroke,
    Such Butchery exhibit ;
Each Arm they maim'd, each Head they topt,
Nor ever left a Limb unlopt,
    To make the Dogs a Gibbet.

So looks the poor difmember'd Tar,
Who late was Thunderbolt of War,
    But fall'n in barb'rous Clutches ;
From mangling Hofpital turn'd out,
Maim'd, halt, and naked, limps about,
    To beg with Stumps and Crutches.

* The Church of St. *Peter* in the Eaft, at *Oxford.*

Oh !

Oh! how the fad fucceeding Year,
Will each kind Stranger's pitying Tear,
   Our wond'rous Change bemoan;
To fee each Tree, once green and tall,
A fhapelefs Block become; and all
   Our Hedge-rows turn'd to Stone.

But we, bleft Minions, all our Days
Shall bafk in *Phæbus'* warmeft Rays,
   No Shade can now controul us:
And fhould he chance to overheat us,
He by the fame good Hand can treat us,
   With gentle Purge to cool us.

E P I G R A M.
O N   A N
O X F O R D   T O A S T,

With fine Eyes, *and a bad* Voice.

L UCETTA's Charms our Hearts furprife
   At once with Love and Wonder;
She bear's Jove's *Lightning* in her *Eyes,*
   But in her *Voice* his *Thunder.*

(109.)

A BALLAD,

To the Tune of—To you fair Ladies now at Land.

Occasioned by a late Copy of Verses on Miss BRICKENDEN'S *going to Newnham by Water; in which were the following Lines:*

" The lofty Trees of Newnham's pendent Wood,
" To meet her seem to rush into the Flood;
" Peep o'er their Fellows Heads to view the Fair.
" Whose Name upon their wounded Barks they bear.
" Repress your amorous Haste; the lovely Maid
" In *Person* deigns to cheer the gloomy Shade."

WHILST you my charming Anna reign,
    Of ev'ry Muse the Theme;
Whose Presence decks with Flowers the Plain,
    With Pride swells Isis' Stream;
May I presume you'll lend an Ear,
To me, your humble Sonnetcer? —— *Fa, la.*

But lest, my Fair, you think me cold,
    Cry pish, and call me rude;
Or think that I dare be so bold,
    My Passion to intrude;
It is not for myself I sue,
'Tis for *some Trees that die for you.* —— *Fa, la.*

Since

Since late on Ifis' filver Flood
    Your fatal Form was feen,
Some lucklefs *Oaks* of *Newnham Wood*,
    Till then full frefh and green,
ı No more their verdant Honours fpread,
But figh for you, and hang their Head. —— *Fa, la.*

'Tis faid, that with a Look moft queer,
    The Dotards peeping ftood ;
No Prieft with more lafcivious Leer,
    Confeffing Nun e'er view'd ;
Nay that they *rufh'd into the Flood.* ——
Were e'er fuch am'rous *Sticks of Wood?* —— *Fa, la.*

How then can all your num'rous Band
    Of Lovers not defpair :
When *Hearts of Oak* could not withftand
    A Face fo wond'rous fair ?
Since in your Breaft no Pity's found,
Tho' Lovers hang, and *Trees are drown'd.*—— *Fa, la.*

In Pity to your Wit, reftrain
    The Lightning of your Eyes ;
Since at each Glance upon the Plain,
    Some bleeding *Foreft* dies :
If you proceed, my lovely Maid,
You'll ruin our *poetic Shade.*—— *Fa, la.*

                                                Well

Well might the Poet's am'rous Song
    Stile you the public Care;
For all our Country 'Squires e'er long,
    Will dread the paffing Fair.
Think what will good Lord *Harcourt* do,
Now *Newnham Woods* are fir'd by you! — *Fa, la.*

On a BEAUTY with ILL QUALITIES.

MISTAKEN Nature here has join'd
    A beauteous Face and ugly Mind;
In vain the faultlefs Features ftrike,
When Soul and Body are unlike;
Pity thofe fnowy Breafts fhould hide
Deceit, and Avarice, and Pride!

    So in rich Jars from *China* brought,
With glowing Colours gayly wrought,
Oftimes the fubtle Spider dwells,
With fecret Venom bloated fwells,
Weaves all his fatal Nets within,
As unfufpected, as unfeen.

A SONG

A SONG *of* SIMILIES.

By the Reverend Dr. BACON.

I'VE THOUGHT; the fair *Clariffa* cries :
What is it like, Sir? — Like your Eyes.
'Tis like a Chair — 'Tis like a Key —
'Tis like a Purge — 'Tis like a Flea —
'Tis like a Beggar — like the Sun —
'Tis like the Dutch — 'Tis like the Moon —
'Tis like a Kilderkin of Ale —
'Tis like a Doctor — like a Whale.

Why are my Eyes, Sir, like a SWORD?
For that's the Thought upon my Word. ——
Ah! witnefs ev'ry Pang I feel;
The Deaths they give their Likenefs tell.

A Sword is like a Chair, you'll find,
Becaufe 'tis *moft an end behind.*
'Tis like a Key, for 'twill undo one;
'Tis like a Purge, for 'twill run through one.
'Tis like a Flea, and Reafon good,
'Tis often drawing human Blood.
Why like a Beggar you fhall hear,
'Tis often borne before the Mayor.

'Tis like the Sun becaufe 'tis gilt,
Befides it travels in a *Belt*.
'Tis like the Dutch we plainly fee,
Becaufe that State, whenever we
A Pufh for our own Int'reft make,
Does inftantly our Sides forfake.
The Moon — Why when all's faid and done,
A Sword is very like the Moon:
For if his Majefty, (God blefs him)
When County Sheriff comes t' addrefs him,
Is pleas'd his Favours to beftow
On him before him kneeling low,
This o'er his Shoulders glitters bright,
And gives the Glory to the Knight.   [*Night.*]
'Tis like a Kilderkin, no Doubt,
For 'tis not long in drawing out.
'Tis like a Doctor, for who will
Difpute a Doctor's Pow'r to kill?
But why a Sword is like a Whale,
Is no fuch eafy Thing to tell.
But fince all Swords are Swords, d'ye fee,
Why let it then a Backfword be:
Which, if well us'd, will feldom fail
To raife up fomewhat like a *Whale*.

H   *The*

The S N I P E.

An H U M O U R O U S B A L L A D.

By the Same.

Tune, — *Abbot of Canterbury.*

I'LL tell you a Story, a Story that true,
A Story that's difmal, yet comical too ;
It is of a Friar, who fome People think,
Tho' as fweet as a Nut, might have dy'd of a Stink.

     Derry down, down, hey derry down.

This Friar would often go out with his Gun,
And tho' no great Markfman, he thought himfelf one ;
For tho' he for ever was wont to mifs Aim,
Still fomething but never himfelf was to blame.

      · Derry down, &c.

It happen'd young Peter, a Friend of the Friar's,
With Legs arm'd with Leather, for fear of the Briars,
Went out with him once, tho' it fignifies not
Where he hired his Gun, or who tick'd for the Shot.

      Derry down, &c.

Away thefe two trudg'd it, o'er Hills and o'er Dales,
They popt at the Partridges, frighten'd the Quails ;
But, to tell you the Truth, no great Mifchief was done,
Save fpoiling the Proverb, *as fure as a Gun.*

      Derry down, &c.

But at length a poor Snipe flew direct in the Way,
In open Defiance, as if he would fay,
" If only the Friar and Peter are there,
" I'll fly where I lift, there's no Reafon to fear."

Derry down, &c.

Tho' little thought he that his Death was fo nigh,
Yet Peter by Chance fetch'd him down from on high ;
His Shot was ramm'd down with a Journal, I wift,
The firft Time he charg'd fo improper with *Mift.*

Derry down, &c.

Then on both Sides the Speeches began to be made,
As — I beg your Acceptance — Oh ! no Sir, indeed —
I beg that you would Sir, — for both wifely knew,
That one Snipe could ne'er be a Supper for two.

Derry down, &c.

What the Friar declin'd in a moft civil Sort,
Peter flipt in his Pocket ; the De'el take him for't !
But were the Truth known, 'twould plainly appear,
He oft-times had found a longer *Bill* there.

Derry down, &c.

Hid in his Pocket the Snipe fafely lay,
While a Week did pafs over his Head, and a Day,
Till the Ropes for a Toaft too offenfive were grown,
And were fmelt out by ev'ry Nofe but his own.

Derry down, &c.

The

The Friar look'd wholefome it muft be agreed,
So no one could fay, whence the Stink fhould proceed;
Where the Stink might be laid, tho' no one could fay,
'Tis certain he brought it and took it away.

Derry down, &c.

At Sight of the Friar began the Perfume,
And fcarce he appear'd but he fcented the Room:
Snuff-boxes were held in the higheft Efteem,
And all the wry Faces were made where he came.

Derry down, &c.

As the Place he was in it was call'd this and that;
In his Room 'twas a Clofe-ftool, or elfe a dead Rat;
In the Fields where he walk'd for fome Carrion 'twas
     gueft;
'Twas a Fart at the *Angel*, and pafs'd for a Jeft.

Derry down, &c.

At length the Sufpicion fell thick on poor Tray,
Till he took to his Heels and with Speed ran away;
Thought the Friar poor Tray I'll remember thee foon,
If I live to grow fweet I will give thee a Bone.

Derry down, &c.

For he knew that poor Tray was moft highly abus'd,
And if any, himfelf, thus deferv'd to be us'd:
For 'twas certainly he, whom elfe could he think;
'Twas certainly he that muft make all the Stink.

Derry down, &c.

So

So when he came Home he fat down on his Bed,
His Elbow at Diftance fupported his Head;
His Body long while like a Pendulum went;
But all he could do did not alter the Scent.
                              Derry down, &c.

Thus hipp'd he got up and pull'd off his Cloaths,
He peep'd in his Breeches and fmelt to his Hofe,
And the very next Morning frefh Cloaths he put on,
All, all but a Waiftcoat, for he had but one.
                              Derry down, &c.

But changing his Cloaths did not alter the Cafe,
And fo he ftunk on for three Weeks and three Days;
Till to fend for a Doctor he thought it moft meet;
For tho' he was not, yet his Life it was fweet.
                              Derry down, &c.

The Doctor he came, felt his Pulfe in a Trice;
Then crept at a Diftance to give his Advice:
But fweating, nor bleeding, nor purging would do,
For inftead of one Stink this only made two.
                              Derry down, &c.

The Friar oft-times to his Glafs would repair,
But to Death he was frighten'd whene'er he came there;
His Eyes were fo funk, and he look'd fo aghaft,
He verily thought he was ftinking his laft.
                              Derry down, &c.

So for Credit he haftens to burn all his Profe,
And into the Fire his Verfes he throws;
When fearching his Pockets to make up the Pile,
He found out the *Snipe*, that had ftunk all the while.

Derry down, &c.

So he hopes you will now think him wholfome again,
Since his Waiftcoat difcovers the Caufe of his Pain :
To conclude, the poor Friar intreats you to note,
That you might have been fweet had you been in his
Coat.

Derry down, &c.

EPIGRAM in MARTIAL.

Literally *Tranflated.* *Lib. 3. Ep. 57.*

CAllidus impofuit nuper mihi Caupo Ravennæ ;
Cum peterem *mixtum*, vendidit ille *merum*.

TRANSLATION.

A Landlord at *Bath* put upon me a queer Hum ;
I afk'd him for *Punch* —— and the Dog gave me
mere Rum.

TABLE

TABLE TALK.

Written in the Year 1745.

By Mr. KIDGELL of HERTFORD COLLEGE.

- - - - *Votum, Timor, Ira, Voluptas,*
Gaudia, Discursus, nostri, Farrago Libelli.
JUVENAL.

WHEN lovely *Cælia* had resign'd
    The dear Delights of Womankind,
And could, without Reluctance, see
The Powers of Talk-inspiring Tea,
Imperial in its last Decay
Glad Mrs. *Betty*'s harmless Prey:
When all the Fountains that supply
The Pools of rich *Quadrille* were dry,
And each promiscuous Fish was seen
Stretch'd on the Pearl-bespangled *Green*;
When *Phœbus* had consign'd his Pow'r
To a mild *Evening*'s cooler Hour,
And lent the Jewels of his Light
T' adorn the *Empress of the Night*,
'Twas solemnly agreed upon
By *Mary* Cook, and Butler *John*,

That

That Supper in the Parlour fhou'd be
With Expedition vaſt as cou'd be ;
For Maſter with Delay was hungry,
And Miſtreſs with Impatience angry.
Swift as the Word the Cloth was laid,
And all was huſh'd while Grace was ſaid,
When Silence once again gave Way
To bring *Diſcourſe* again in play.
  " But, Sir, if theſe Accounts are true,
The *Dutch* have mighty Things in View ;
The *Auſtrians* —— I admire *French-Beans*,
Dear Ma'em, above all Sorts of Greens,——
They ſay the *Pruſſian* Schemes are quaſh'd ——
Oh Ma'em, 'tis admirably haſh'd ——
Some Pepper —— and I hear *Argyle* ——
A little Vinegar and Oil ——
But that, perhaps, is all a Jeſt, Sir ——
Ma'em, which you pleaſe — which you like beſt Sir —
I think green Peas —— if underſtood
The *Grand Duke's* Schemes —— are lovely good —
Mix'd, Mr. *John* —— will humble *France* ——
Sir, your good Health —— but that's a Chance —
Miſs *Harriot's* vaſtly grown, Ma'em —— why,
So her Papa thinks —— Mrs. *Fry*
Is out of Patience —— Ma'em a Piece
Of Sturgeon —— with her *little* Niece,
They're

They're both Year's Children — *John*, some Bread —
But *Harriot's taller* by the Head.
She came from School, stay, let me see,
I think 'twas —— Almond Flummery,
Venture to taste it, Mr. *Sear* ————
The Night that *Garrick* play'd King *Lear*.
Oh, I remember! —— Dearest Ma'em, let
Me help you —— when he acted *Hamlet*
My Sister *Ashburnham* had on
Her Pink and Silver —— Hark'ee, *John* ——
And some rude Rabble from the Gallery ——
The Soup tastes delicate of Celery ——
Threw God knows what upon her Sleeve ——
She's got it out, Ma'em, I perceive. ——
Oh, no, Ma'em, she was forc'd to buy
(Your humble Servant, Dr. *Dry*)
A whole new Breadth —— we had such Sport ——
Of Mrs. *Vokes* in *Old Round Court*.
Dear Mrs. *Chatwell*, have you heard ——
To me a Teal's a better Bird ————
How Mrs. *Branche's* Cause goes on?
A little Water, Mr. *John* ——
O! Mrs. *Branche!* I can't abide her ——
Pray, Mr. *James*, a Glass of Cyder.
Some say —— a little Butter mix'd
With Capers —— she is so unfix'd,

She

She can't —— eats moſt delightful in it ——
Continue in a Mind one Minute. ——
No! Carp, Ma'em, is —— and ſo we ſee ——
Above all Sorts of Fiſh to me ——
A Triflingneſs —— you knew *Tom*'s Wife ——
In every Action of her Life ——
Tom Branche's Wife I knew —— another
Potatoe if you pleaſe —— and Mother.
His Mother —— Mr. *Oldham* ſpeaks,
John, don't you hear? —— within three Weeks
After —— Theſe Eggs I always poach ——
Was overturn'd in *York* Stage-Coach ——
And Mrs. *Mixon*, as for her ——
Miſs, your good Health, Ma'em, your's, good Sir, ——
She went to *Perth* —— poor Soul, it cry'd,
And ran to me —— and there ſhe dy'd ——
Poor little Soul! Ma'em, ſome of thoſe ——
And did it hurt its little Noſe! ——
Yes, Ma'em, it bled —— I chuſe a Wing,
Sir, you are quite —— like any Thing.
But Doctor, if the noble Duke ——
Take out that Skew'r there to the Cook ——
Shou'd trounce Monſieur, I'm bold to ſay ——
A little Sweet-Bread, Mrs. *Day* ——
That 'tis impoſſible the *Dutch* ——
Ma'em, if you pleaſe, not quite ſo much ——

Refuſe

Refuse t' affift —— Yes, Ma'em, but Spices
Improve it vaftly —— at this Crifis. ——
Good gracious! He's a dreadful Jobfter ——
Ma'em, I prefer one Inch of Lobfter ——
He piec'd my Habit all in Dabs ——
At any Time to twenty Crabs ——
Oh! I'd forgot —— they're lovely Rabbits,
Dear Ma'em! —— but now you mention Habits,
Mifs *Drawbridge*—Your good Health, Mifs *Perkin* —
Has got the fearful'ft, frightful'ft Jerkin,
It looks fo tarnifh'd and fo old ——
Mifs *Jewkes*, I hope you've caught no Cold ——
No, not at all, Ma'em — Fetch the Cheefe in ——
Snuff always did fet me a fneezing ——
The Affociation's form'd we hear ——
John, mix a little Ale and Beer ——
Why, really, Ma'em — your Health, Mifs *Bayes* —
Folks talk on't many different Ways ——
Tho' 'tis a Cafe that I'm no Judge in ——
Ma'em, I'm prodigious fond of Gudgeon ——
But apt to prate —— they're fine ftew'd Pears ——
At fuch a Juncture of Affairs.
Dear Ma'em, you've heard how 'Squire *Codling* —
My Daughter *Ford* admires a Codling ——
It rain'd fo dreadful cou'd not go,
He and Mifs *James*, and Mrs. *Sloc*,

So

So far as *Tewkſbury* laſt Week ———

Sure, *John*, you heard Miſs *Idle* ſpeak !

You ſaw Miſs *Drawbridge*, Ma'em, laſt *Sunday?*

Yes, Ma'em, 1 did; and Mrs. *Munday*

Had loſt her Parrot —— Pray, Ma'em, how ?

I really, Ma'em, can't tell, I vow ———

I pity'd the poor Creature's Fate ———

Give Mrs. *Dykes* a China Plate ———

But poor Miſs *Drawbridge* will run wild ———

No, Ma'em, our Cream is always boil'd ———

For our Part, Ma'em, I can't but ſay

We all —— make Haſte and take away ——

Are mighty fond of Slip-flops —— bring

The Wine and Fruits — Ma'em, *Church* and *King* —

Miſs, ſhall I help you ? Sir, I beg ——

Sir, there's enough —— Ma'em, Siſter *Peg*

Is well, but *George* has hurt his Leg :

My Aunt was in a vehement Fright ———

His left Leg, Ma'em — No, Ma'em, his right ——

Poor Maſter *Gregory !* —— Ma'em, I hope ——

No, Ma'em, he's with my Uncle *Cope*,

And is as lively and as briſk

As —— Ma'em do you chuſe a Game at Whiſk ?

SIMILE,

S I M I L E,

From PHÆDRA and HYPPOLITUS.

SO when bright Venus yielded up her Charms,
   The bleſt Adonis languiſh'd in her Arms:
His idle Horn on fragrant Myrtles hung,
His Arrows ſcatter'd, and his Bow unſtrung.
Obſcure in Coverts lay his dreaming Hounds,
And bay'd the fancy'd Boar with feeble Sounds;
For nobler Sports he quits the ſavage Fields,
And all the Hero to the Lover yields.

The Same PARODIED.

SO when bright Abigail reſign'd her Charms,
   The happy Curate languiſh'd in her Arms:
His unbruſh'd Beaver on the Floor was toſs'd;
His Notes were ſcatter'd, and his Bible loſt.
In Alehouſe hid this dreaming Clerk was found,
And rear'd the fancy'd Stave with feeble Sound:
For nobler Sheets his Concordance he leaves,
And all the Parſon to the Lover gives.

VERSES

V E R S E S

ON THE

Expected Arrival of Queen CHARLOTTE,

In an EPISTLE to a FRIEND, 1761.

By a GENTLEMAN of OXFORD.

Containing the *Sentiments*, *Images*, *Metaphors*, *Machinery*, *Similies*, *Allufions*, and all other Poetical *Decorations*, of the OXFORD VERSES, which were to appear on that aufpicious Occafion.

YES — every hopeful Son of Rhyme
 Will furely feize this happy Time,
Vault upon Pegafus's Back,
Now grown an Academick Hack,
And fing the Beauties of a Queen,
(Whom, by the bye, he has not feen;)
Will fwear her Eyes are black as Jet,
Her Teeth are Pearls in Coral fet;
Will tell us that the Rofe has lent
Her Cheek its Bloom, her Lips its Scent,
That Philomel breaks off her Song,
And liftens to her fweeter Tongue;

That

That Venus and the Graces join'd
To form this Phœnix of her Kind,
And Pallas undertook to ſtore
Her Mind with Wiſdom's chiefeſt Lore :
Thus form'd, Jove iſſues a Decree
That GEORGE's Conſort ſhe ſhall be :
Then Cupid (for what Match is made
By Poets without Cupid's Aid ?)
Picks out the ſwifteſt of his Darts,
And pierces inſtant both their Hearts.

    Your fearful Proſe-men here might doubt
How beſt to bring this Match about,
For Winds and Waves are ill-bred Things,
And little care for Queens and Kings ;
But as the Gods aſſembled ſtand,
And wait each youthful Bard's Command,
All fancy'd Dangers they deride,
Of boiſt'rous Winds, and ſwelling Tide ;
Neptune is call'd to wait upon her,
And Sea-Nymphs are her Maids of Honour ;
Whilſt we, inſtead of eaſtern Gales,
With Vows and Praiſes fill the Sails,
And when, with due poetic Care
They ſafely land the Royal Fair,
They catch the happy Simile,
Of Venus riſing from the Sea.

Soon

Soon as she moves, the Hill and Vale;
Refponfive tell the joyful Tale ;
And Wonder holds th' enraptur'd Throng
To fee the Goddefs pafs along ;
The bowing Forefts all adore her,
And Flow'rs fpontaneous fpring before her,
Where you and I all Day might travel,
And meet with nought but Sand and Gravel;
But Poets have a piercing Eye,
And many pretty Things can fpy,
Which neither you nor I can fee,
But then the Fault's in you and me.
The King aftonifh'd muft appear,
And find that Fame has wrong'd his Dear;
Then Hymen, like a Bifhop, ftands,
To join the Lovers' plighted Hands;
Apollo and the Mufes wait,
The nuptial Song to celebrate.
    But I, who rarely fpend my Time
In paying Court or fpinning Rhyme ;
Who cannot from the high Abodes,
Call down, at Will, a Troop of Gods;
Muft in the plain profaick Way,
The Wifhes of my Soul convey.
May Heaven our Monarch's Choice approve,
May he be bleft with mutual Love,

And

And be as happy with his Queen,
As with my Chloe I have been;
When wand'ring through the Beechen Grove,
She fweetly fmil'd and talk'd of Love!
And oh! that he may live to fee
A Son as wife and good as he;
And may his Confort grace the Throne
With Virtues equal to his own!
Our courtly Bards will needs be telling,
That fhe's like Venus or like Helen;
I wifh that fhe may prove as fair
As Egremont and Pembroke are;
For tho' by Sages 'tis confeft,
That Beauty's but a Toy at beft;
Yet, 'tis methinks, in married Life,
A pretty Douceur with a Wife:
And may the Minutes as they fly,
Strengthen ftill the nuptial Tye,
While Hand in Hand thro' Life they go,
'Till Love fhall into Friendfhip grow;
For tho' thefe Bleffings rarely wait
On regal Pomp, and tinfel'd State,
Yet Happinefs is Virtue's Lot,
Alike in Palace and in Cot:
'Tis true, the grave Affairs of State,
With little Folks have little Weight;

I   Yet

Yet I confefs my Patriot Heart
In Britain's Welfare bears its Part;
With Tranfport glows at GEORGE's Name,
And triumphs in its Country's Fame:
With hourly Pleafure I can fit
And talk of *Granby*, *Hawk*, and *Pitt*;
And whilft I praife the Good and Brave,
Difdain the Coward and the Knave.
At Growth of Taxes others fret,
And fhudder at the Nation's Debt;
I ne'er the fancied Ills bemoan,
No Debts difturb me, but my own.
What! tho' our Coffers fink, our Trade
Repairs the Breach which War has made.;
And if Expences now run high,
Our Minds muft with our Means comply.
Thus far my Politicks extend,
And here my warmeft Wifhes end,
May Merit flourifh, Faction ceafe,
And I and Europe live in Peace!

ODE to CRITICISM.*

By Mr. WODHULL.

Mutemus Clypeos, Danaumque Infignia Nobis
Aptemus. Dolus, an Virtus, quis in Hofte requirit ? Virgil.

I.

HAIL, mighty Goddefs, whom of yore,
   Where fam'd Cimmeria boafts her tenfold Gloom,
In thofe deep Caverns, from her lab'ring Womb
      Imperial Dulnefs bore.
    At the Signal of thy Birth,
    O'er the Rue-befprinkled Earth,
Slowly fullen Spleen advances,
   Sneering Laughter joins the Dances,
Swift from her Den exulting Envy fprings,
New trims her faded Torch, and fharpens all her Stings.

II.

   Farewel, ye Vifions light and vain,
The Delian Grove, with its enchanted Rill,
The cloven Summits of Parnaffus' Hill,
    Chimeras of the Brain.

---

* This Poem appeared foon after the Publication of the *Ox-*
ford Verfes on the Death of his late Majefty.

        No

No more fuch Follies I purfue ————

'Thee, fober-vefted Queen, I woo ;

Thy propitious Help imploring,

As by Midnight Taper poring,

With ftudious Care I mark fome faulty Line,

Then curfe the Theban Harp, or *Homer's* Work divine.

III.

Here in my hateful, lonefome Cell,

While Darknefs fpreads her murky Veil around,

When Pains corode, and ftormy Paffions wound,

. With thee I wifh to dwell.

Tho' *Apollo* bids defpair,

Nor a Mufe regards my Pray'r ;

Still with ever conftant Kindnefs,

Thou wilt footh my votive Blindnefs ;

I feel, I feel the maddening Influence reigns,

The black Bile rufhes on, and revels in my Veins.

IV.

Borne on the rapid Wings of Thought,

E'en now I feem, in thy extenfive Shade,

Where baleful Yew's o'ercome the fickening Glade,

To quaff the plenteous Draught,

And behold thy Realms comprife

Learned, Ignorant, and Wife,

All alike with hot Devotion,

Swallowing thy embitter'd Potion.

Fearlefs

Fearlefs I take my felf-commiffion'd Stand,
To wield thy ruthlefs Sword with unrelenting Hand.

V.

Hear then, O hear my fond Requeft,
Whether in poor *Verona's* haplefs State,
Thou mourn'ft thy *Scaliger's* neglected Fate,
   With Anguifh-laden Breaft.
Or with Rapture lov'ft to view
  Sourly fmiling each *Review*;
  Quickly hafte to my Embraces,
  Come, O come, in all thy Graces,
Where tuneful *Oxford hails* thy *juft* Domain,
Where at thy Shrine attend her delegated Train.

VI.

How fhall I paint thy heavenly Charms!
In what high Praife my ardent Suit addrefs!
Or how the glowing Flame fhall I exprefs
   Which now my Bofom warms;
  How defcribe the mazy Road,
  Leading to thy bleft Abode!
  Where thou fit'ft in State prefiding,
  Us ignoble Rhimers guiding
To where the Banks of *Lethe's* filent Wave,
Before our paffive Steps difclofe an early Grave.

Yet

VII.

Yét fhall my feeble Lays prefume,.
Rapt in ideal Extacies, to trace
The winning Features of thy lovely Face,
    And its primeval Bloom.
Thou, a *Silver flipper'd* Nymph *,
    Lightly tread'ft the *dimply* Lymph,
With dank Sedge thy Treffes wreathing,
Modulated Meafures breathing;
A *Coral Crown* thy *Bright Brow binds*, I ween,
And down devolves thy *Sweeping Stole of Gloffy Green*.

VIII.

Oft, in noctarnal Serenade,
Anxious I wake my Lyre's difcordant Strings,
Till the refponfive Echo loudly rings
    With thee, immortal Maid!
Ah! perchance my Hopes are vain ——
Canft thou then with harfh Difdain,

---

* Alluding to the following Lines in *Warton's* TRIUMPH
OF ISIS.
And from the Wave arofe its guardian Queen,
Known by her fweeping Stole of gloffy Green;
While in the coral Crown that bound her Brow,
Was wove the Delphic Laurel's verdant Bough.
As the fmooth Surface of the dimply Flood,
The Silver-flippered ISIS lightly trod.

Spurn

Spurn my too officious Duty,
Self-enamour'd of thy Beauty;
And clofe thy ftern, inexorable Heart,
Slighting the Vow fincere, which wants the Glofs of Art.

IX.

Hence, idle Fears ——— thou ftill art kind;
Low at thy Footftool bends my trembling Knee;
I fue, O Goddefs, and I fue to thee,
    To thy Behefts refign'd.
  No rejected Votary's Moans
  Taint the Air with feverifh Groans.
Where we reft, thy Charms enjoying,
Ever tafted, never cloying,
Widely thou pour'ft thy all-diffufive Rays,
Inftant our kindling Souls with Fire congenial blaze.

X.

In *Rhedycina*'s favour'd Seat,
Where richeft Verfe thy fmould'ring Altar feeds,
With him fome chofen Sage obedient leads,
    To give 'Thee Homage meet.
  Falfe Surmifes, hidden Flaws,
  Old Grammarians crabbed Laws;
At thy Impulfe while clated,
By thy Pleafure he unfated,
With his fell Pen from thy Tribunal bends,
As on the mangled Lines the frequent Blot defcends.

          When

XI.

When Autumn brought the lowering Year,
Fair *Isis* mingled with *Britannia*'s Woe;
Meanwhile thou taught'ft her Claffic Plaints to flow
O'er *George*'s Grief-ftrain'd Bier.
How fhe mourn'd the Monarch dead,
Father of his Country fled,
Ill befits my trite Narration ——
I in lefs exalted Station,
Stupidly nod o'er Poefy fo fine,
Stretch'd on the lifelefs Couch of Indolence fupine.

XII.

That Part to Thee we confecrate
Of the huge *Wreath* forfooth, *which all the Nine,*
*With Skill united have confpir'd to twine.**
A Fricaffee of State !
'Twould make a Breakfaft for a King;
Or fhould he feaft on no fuch Thing
As See-faw Flattery, and his Spirit
Be cooly touch'd with fo much Merit;

* Alluding to the following Lines in the concluding Copy of
the Oxford Verses above-mentioned, written by the Poetry
Profeffor.
- - - - - - - - - deign to view
This ample Wreath, which all th' affembled Nine
With Skill united have confpir'd to twine.

If

If he endure the Song with Look finister,
The Plan will fuit at leaft a Patriot-Minifter.

XIII.

Full many a Youth, whofe opening Shoot
Teem'd with Poetic Foliage, o'er whofe Head
Caftalian Dews the gracious Mufe has fhed,
    And promis'd riper Fruit;
   Such the firm Decrees of Fate,
   Such the Shortnefs of his Date,
  With the Troop of Phantoms namelefs,
  In that pious Volume famelefs,
Where the triumphant Clouds of Smoke afpire,
Sinks in Oblivion's Arms on the funereal Pyre.

XIV.

Far from the Terrors of thy Reign,
Curb'd by thy Frown, audacious Genius flies;
Or, if he impotently dares to rife,
    Is levell'd to the Plain:
   Nought avails his magic Art
   To avert thy vengeful Dart;
  And his infolent emprifing;
  Thou his vaunting Pow'r defpifing,
Eager his blafted Glories to confound,
Strik'ft him a breathlefs Corfe, unpitying, to the Ground.

                         When

XV.

When † *Swinging Slow with Sweepy Sway*,
In one fame conftant Tenor run our Rhimes,
Like the fweet Mufick of unvaried Chimes,
    In diftant due Delay ;
    Then our Vows thou deign'ft to hear
    With a condefcending Ear.
    Aid, O Goddefs, aid my Numbers,
    Let me *ſhare* thy *Sweeteſt Slumbers*,
While from this Quill, as all along I doze,
In Apathy difcreet the ftumbling Stanza flows.

† See WARTON's *Pleaſures of Melancholy*, a Poem.

A N

IMITATION of SPENSER.

I.

A Well-known Vase of sovraign Use I sing,
    Pleasing to Young and Old, and *Jordan* hight.
The lovely Queen, and eke the haughty King
Snatch up this Vessel in the murky Night;
Ne lives there poor, ne lives there wealthy Wight,
But uses it in mantle brown or green;
Sometimes it stands array'd in glossy white;
And eft in mighty Dortours may be seen.
Of China's fragile Earth, with azure Flowrets sheen.

II.

The Virgin comely as the dewy Rose,
Here gently sheds the softly-whisp'ring Rill;
The Frannion, who ne Shame ne Blushing knows,
At once the Potter's glossy Vase does fill;
It whizzes like the Waters from a Mill.
Here frouzy Housewives clear their loaded Reins;
The Beef-fed Justice, who fat Ale doth swill,
Grasps the round-handled Jar, and tries, and strains,
While slowly dribbling down the scanty Water drains.

The

III.

The Dame of Fraunce fhall without Shame convey
This ready Needment to its proper Place;
Yet fhall the Daughters of the Lond of Fay
Learn better Amenaunce and decent Grace;
Warm Blufhes lend a Beauty to their Face,
For Virtue's comely Tints their Cheeks adorn;
Thus o'er the diftant Hillocks you may trace
The purple Beamings of the infant Morn:
Sweet are our blooming Maids —— the fweeteft Crea-
   tures born.

IV.

None but their Hufbands or their Lovers true
They truft with Management of their Affairs;
Nor even thefe their Privacy may view,
When the foft Beavies feek the Bow'r by Pairs:
Then from the Sight accoy'd, like tim'rous Hares,
From Mate or Bellamour alike they fly;
Think not, good Swain, that thefe are fcornful Airs,
Think not for Hate they fhun thine am'rous Eye,
Soon fhall the Fair return, nor done thee, Youth, to dye.

V.

While Belgic Frows acrofs a Charcoal Stove
(Replenifh'd like the Veftal's lafting Fire)
Bren for whole Years, and fcorch the Parts of Love,
No longer Parts that can Delight infpire,

Erft

Erft Cave of Blifs, now monumental Pyre;
O British Maid, for ever clean and neat,
For whom I aye will wake my fimple Lyre,
With double Care preferve that dun Retreat,
Fair Venus' myftic Bow'r, Dan Cupid's feather'd Seat.

VI.

So may your Hours foft-fliding fteal away,
Unknown to gnarring Slander and to Bale,
O'er Seas of Blifs. Peace guides her Gondelay,
Ne bitter Dole impeft the paffing Gale.
O fweeter than the Lilies of the Dale,
In your foft Breafts the Fruits of Joyance grow.
Ne fell Defpair be here with Vifage pale,
Brave be the Youth for whom your Bofoms glow,
Ne other Joy but you the faithful Striplings know.

A N

An Excellent BALLAD.

To the Tune of *Chevy-Chace*.

WHilome there dwelt near *Buckingham*,
   That famous Country Town,
At a known Place, hight *Whaddon Chace*,
   A Squire of odd Renown. ——

A Druid's facred Form he bore,
   His Robes a Girdle bound:
Deep vers'd he was in antient Lore,
   In Cuftoms old, profound.

A Stick torn from that hallow'd Tree,
   Where *Chaucer* us'd to fit,
And tell his Tales with leering Glee,
   Supports his tott'ring Feet.

High on a Hill his Manfion ftood,
   But gloomy dark within;
Here mangled Books, as Bones and Blood
   Lie in a Giant's Den.

Crude, undigefted, half-devour'd,
   On groaning Shelves they're thrown;
Such Manufcripts no Eye could read,
   Nor Hand write — but his own.

No Prophet He, like Sydrophel,
 Could future Times explore;
But what had happen'd, he could tell,
 Five hundred Years and more.

A walking Alm'nack he appears,
 Stept from some mouldy Wall,
Worn out of Use thro' Dust and Years,
 Like Scutcheons in his Hall.

His Boots were made of that Cow's Hide,
 By *Guy of Warwick* slain;
Time's choicest Gifts, aye to abide
 Among the chosen Train.

Who first receiv'd the precious Boon,
 We're at a Loss to learn,
By *Spelman, Cambden, Dugdale,* worn,
 And then they came to *Hearne.*

Hearne, strutted in them for awhile;
 And then, as lawful Heir,
Brown claim'd and seiz'd the precious Spoil,
 The Spoil of many a Year.

His Car himself he did provide,
 To stand in double Stead;
That it should carry him alive,
 And bury him when dead.

By

By rufty Coins old Kings he'd trace,
  And know their Air and Mien :
King *Alfred* he knew well by Face,
  Tho' *George* he ne'er had feen.

This Wight th' outfide of Churches lov'd,
  Almoft unto a Sin ;
Spires Gothic of more Ufe he prov'd
  Than Pulpits are within.

Of ufe, no doubt, when high in Air,
  A wand'ring Bird they'll reft,
Or with a Bramin's holy Care,
  Make Lodgments for its Neft.

Ye Jackdaws, that are us'd to talk,
  Like us of human Race,
When nigh you fee *Brown Willis* walk,
  Loud chatter forth his Praife.

Whene'er the fatal Day fhall come,
  For come, alas ! it muft,
When this good 'Squire muft ftay at home,
  And turn to antique Duft ;

The folemn Dirge, ye Owls, prepare,
  Ye Bats, more hoarfly fcreak ;
Croak, all ye Ravens, round the Bier,
  And all ye Church-mice, fqueak !

A

D I A L O G U E

BETWEEN

The POET and his SERVANT.

In Imitation of HORACE, Sat. ix. Book ii.

By the late Mr. CHRISTOPHER PITT.

Serv. SIR,—I've long waited, in my Turn, to have
A Word with you—but I'm your humble Slave.
Poet. What Knave is that? my Rafcal!
                              Servant. Sir, 'tis I,
No Knave, nor Rafcal, but your trufty *Guy.*
    Poet. Well, as your Wages ftill are due, I'll bear
Your damn'd Impertinence, this Time of Year.
    Serv. Some Folks are drunk one Day, and fome for
        ever,
And fome, like *H******,* but twelve Years together.
Old *Evremond,* renown'd for Wit and Dirt,
Would change his Living, oft'ner than his Shirt;
Roar with the Rakes of State a Month, and come
To ftarve another in his Hole at Home.
So rov'd wild *Buckingham,* the publick Jeft,
Now fome Inn-holder's, now a Monarch's Gueft;

K   His

His Life and Politicks of ev'ry Shape,
This Hour a *Roman*, and the next an Ape.
The Gout in ev'ry Limb from ev'ry Vice,
Poor *N****** hir'd a Boy to throw the Dice.
Some wench forever; — and their Sins in thofe
By Cuftom fit as eafy as their Clothes.
Some fly like Pendulums from Good to Evil,
And in that Point are madder than the Devil:
For they ——

    Poet. To what will thefe wife Maxims tend?
And where, fweet Sir, will your Reflections end?

    Serv. In you.

    Poet. In me, you Knave, make out your Charge.

    Serv. You praife low living, but you live at large.
Perhaps you fcarce believe the Rules you teach,
Or find it hard to practife what you preach.
Scarce have you paid one idle Journey down,
But without Bus'nefs you're again in Town.
If none invite you, Sir, abroad to roam,
Then — Lord, what Pleafure 'tis to read at home!
And fip your two Half-pints with great Delight
Of Beer at Noon, and muddled Port at Night.
From *Encombe*, *John* comes thund'ring at the Door,
With — Sir, my Mafter begs you to come o'er,
To pafs the tedious Hours, thefe Winter Nights;
Not that he dreads Invafions, Rogues, or Sprites.—

                          Strait

Strait for your two beſt Wigs aloud you call,
This ſtiff in Buckle, that not curl'd at all.
And where the Devil are the Spurs? you cry,
And Pox! what Blockhead laid the Buſkins by?
On your old batter'd Mare you'll needs be gone,
(No matter whether on four Legs or none)
Splaſh, plunge, and ſtumble, as you ſcour the Heath,
All ſwear at *Morden* 'tis on Life and Death:
As fierce through *Wareham* Streets you ſcamper on,
Raiſe all the Dogs and Voters in the Town;
Then fly for ſix long dirty Miles as bad,
That *Corfe* and *Kingſton* Gentry think you mad.
And all this furious Riding is to prove
Your high Reſpect, it ſeems, and eager Love:
And yet that mighty Honour to obtain,
Banks, Shaftſbury, Dodington, may ſend in vain.
Before you go, we curſe the Noiſe you make,
And bleſs the Moment that you turn your Back.
Meantime your Flock, depriv'd of heav'nly Food,
As we of carnal, ſtarve and ſtray abroad:
Left to your Care by Providence in vain,
You leave them all to Providence again.
As for myſelf, I own it to your Face,
I love good Eating,——and I take my Glaſs:
But ſure 'tis ſtrange, dear Sir, that one ſhould be
In you Amuſement, but a Crime in me.

All

All this is bare refining on a Name,
To make a Difference where the Fault's the same.
My Father fold me to your Service here,
For this fine Livery, and four Pounds a Year.
A Livery you fhould wear as well as I,
And this I'll prove, — but lay your Cudgel by.
You ferve your Paffions. Thus, without a Jeft,
Both are but Fellow-fervants at the beft.
Yourfelf, good Sir, are play'd by your Defires,
A meer tall Poppet dancing on the Wires.

   Poet. Who at this Rate of talking can be free?
   Serv. The brave, wife, honeft Man, and only he:
All elfe are Slaves alike, the World around,
Kings on the Throne, and Beggars on the Ground.
He, Sir, is Proof to Grandeur, Pride, or Pelf,
And (greater ftill) is Mafter of himfelf:
Not to and fro' by Fears and Factions hurl'd,
But loofe to all the Interefts of the World:
And while the World turns round, entire and whole
He keeps the facred Tenour of his Soul;
In every Turn of Fortune ftill the fame,
As Gold unchang'd, or brighter from the Flame:
Collected in himfelf, with godlike Pride,
He fees the Darts of Envy glance afide;
And fix'd like *Atlas*, while the Tempefts blow,
Smiles at the idle Storms that roar below.

One

One such you know, a Layman to your Shame,
And yet the Honour of your Blood and Name.
If you can such a Character maintain,
You too are free, — and I'm your Slave again.
But when in *Brun*'s feign'd Battles you delight
More than myself to see two Drunkards fight,
Fool, Rogue, Sot, Blockhead, or such Names are
      mine,
Yours are a Connoiffeur, or deep Divine.
I'm chid for loving a luxurious Bit,
The sacred Prize of Learning, Worth, and Wit:
And yet some fell their Lands thefe Bits to buy;
Then pray who suffers moft from Luxury!
I'm chid, 'tis true; but then I pawn no Plate,
I feal no Bonds, I mortgage no Eftate.
Befides high Living, Sir, muft wear you out
With Surfeits, Qualms, a Fever, or the Gout.
By some new Pleafures are you ftill engrofs'd,
And when you fave an Hour you think it loft.
To Sports, Plays, Races, from your Books you run,
And like all Company except your own.
You hunt, drink, fleep, or (idler ftill) you rhyme:
Why? — but to banifh Thought, and murder Time.
And yet that Thought which you difcharge in vain,
Like a foul-loaded Piece, recoils again.

Poet. *Tom,* fetch a Cane, a Whip, a Club, a Stone. —
Servant. For What?

             Poet. A Sword, a Piftol, or a Gun.
I'll fhoot the Dog.

             Serv. Lord, who would be a Wit?
He's in a mad, or in a rhyming Fit.

   Poet. Fly, fly, you Rafcal, for your Spade and Fork;
For once I'll fet your lazy Bones to work.
Fly, or I'll fend you back without a Groat
To the bleak Mountains where you firft were caught.

E P I G R A M,

On *the Rev. Mr.* Hanbury's PLANTATIONS *and* MUSIC MEETING, *at* Church-Langton, *in* Leicefterfhire.

S O fweet thy *Strain,* fo thick thy *Shade,*
    The pleas'd Spe&ctator fees
The Miracle once more difplay'd
    Of *Orpheus* and his *Trees.*

                        THE

THE

LAW-STUDENT.

To George Colman, A. M. of Ch. Ch. Oxford.

Quid tibi cum Cirrhâ? quid cum Permeſſidos undâ?
Romanum proprius divitiuſque Forum eſt. MARTIAL.

NOW Chriſt-Church left, and fixt at Lincoln's Inn,
  Th' important Studies of the Law begin.
Now groan the Shelves beneath th' unuſual Charge
Of Records, Statutes, and Reports at large.
Each claſſic Author ſeeks his peaceful Nook,
And modeſt Virgil yields his Place to *Coke*,
No more, ye Bards, for vain Precedence hope,
But even *Jacob* take the Lead of *Pope!*

While the pil'd Shelves ſink down on one another,
And each huge Folio has it's cumb'rous Brother,
While, arm'd with theſe, the Student views with Awe
His Rooms become the Magazine of Law,
Say whence ſo few ſucceed? where thouſands aim,
So few e'er reach the promis'd Goal of Fame?
Say, why *Cæcilius* quits the gainful Trade
For Regimentals, Sword, and ſmart Cockade?

Or

Or *Sextus* why his firft Profeffion leaves
For narrower Band, plain Shirt, and pudding Sleeves?

The Depth of Law afks Study, Thought and Care?
Shall we feek thefe in rich *Alonzo*'s Heir?
Such Diligence, alas! is feldom found
In the brifk Heir to forty thoufand Pound.
Wealth, that excufes Folly, Sloth creates,
Few, who can fpend, e'er learn to get Eftates.
What is to him dry Cafe, or dull Report,
Who ftudies Fafhions at the Inns of Court;
And proves that Thing of Emptinefs and Show,
That Mungrel, half-form'd Thing, a Temple-Beau?
Obferve him daily fauntring up and down,
In purple Slippers, and in filken Gown;
Laft Night's Debauch, his Morning Converfation,
The Coming, all his Evening Preparation.

By Law let others toil to gain Renown!
Florio's a Gentleman, a Man o'th' Town.
He nor Courts, Clients, or the Law regarding,
Hurries from Nando's down to Covent-Garden.
Yet he's a Scholar; — mark him in the Pit
With Critic Catcall found the Stops of Wit!
Supreme at George's he harangues the Throng,
Cenfor of Style from Tragedy to Song:

Him

Him ev'ry Witling views with fecret Awe,
Deep in the Drama, fhallow in the Law.

Others there are, who, indolent and vain,
Contemn the Science they can ne'er attain :
Who write and read, but all by Fits and Starts,
And varnifh Folly with the Name of Parts;
Truft on to Genius, for they fcorn to pore,
'Till e'en that little Genius is no more.

Knowledge in Law Care only can attain,
Where Honour's purchas'd at the Price of Pain.
If, loit'ring, up the Afcent you ceafe to climb,
No Starts of Labour can redeem the Time.
Induftrious Study wins by flow Degrees,
True Sons of *Coke* can ne'er be Sons of Eafe.

There are, whom Love of Poetry has fmit,
Who, blind to Intereft, arrant Dupes to Wit,
Have wander'd devious in the pleafing Road,
With Attic Flowers and Claffic Wreaths beftrew'd :
Wedded to Verfe, embrac'd the Mufe for Life,
And ta'en, like modern Bucks, their Whores to Wife.
Where'er the Mufe ufurps defpotic Sway,
All other Studies muft of Force give Way.
Int'reft in vain puts in her prudent Claim,
Nonfuited by the pow'rful Plea of Fame.

As well you might weigh Lead againſt a Feather,
As ever jumble Wit anu Law together.
On *Littleton, Coke* gravely thus Remarks,
(Remember this, ye rhyming Temple Sparks!)
" In all our Author's Tenures, be it noteᴅ,
" This is the fourth Time any Verſe is quoted."
Which, 'gainſt the Muſe and Verſe, may well imply
What Lawyers call a *Noli Proſcqui.*

Quit then, dear *George*, O quit the barren Field,
Which neither Profit nor Reward can yield !
What tho' the ſprightly Scene, well acted, draws
From unpack'd Engliſhmen, unbrib'd Applauſe,
Some monthly Grub, ſome *Dennis* of the Age,
In print cries Shame on the degen'rate Stage *.
If haply *Churchill* ſtrive, with generous Aim,
To fan the Sparks of Genius to a Flame ;
If all ᴜɴᴀꜱᴋ'ᴅ, ᴜɴᴋɴᴏᴡɪɴɢ, and ᴜɴᴋɴᴏᴡɴ,
By noting thy Deſert, he prove his own ;
Envy ſhall ſtrait to *Hamilton*'s Repair,
And vent her Spleen, and Gall, and Venom there,

---

* Alluding to certain diſingenuous and illiberal Criticiſms in the *Critical Review*; wherein the *Jealous Wife*, a Comedy, and the Author of that Play, as well as his Friends, were at different Times attacked, with equal Virulence and Inſolence.

Thee

Thee, and thy Works, and all thy Friends decry,
And boldly print and publiſh a rank Lie,
Swear your own Hand the flatt'ring Likeneſs drew,
Swear your own Breath Fame's partial Trumpet blew.

Well I remember oft your Friends have ſaid,
(Friends whom the ſureſt Maxims ever led)
Turn Parſon, *Colman*, that's the Way to thrive;
Your Parſons are the happieſt Men alive.
Judges, there are but Twelve, and never more,
But Stalls untold, and Biſhops, Twenty-four.
Of Pride and Claret, Sloth and Ven'ſon full,
Yon Prelate mark, Right Reverend and dull!
He ne'er, good Man, need penſive Vigils keep
To preach his Audience once a Week to ſleep;
On rich Preferments battens at his Eaſe,
Nor ſweats for Tithes, as Lawyers toil for Fees.

Thus they advis'd. I know thee better far;
And cry, ſtick cloſe, dear *Colman*, to the Bar!
If Genius warm thee, where can Genius call
For nobler Action than in yonder Hall?
'Tis not enough each Morn, on Term's Approach,
To club your legal Three-pence for a Coach;
Then at the Hall to take your ſilent Stand,
With Ink-horn and long Note-book in your Hand,

Marking

Marking grave Serjeants cite each wife Report,
And noting down fage Dictums from the Court,
With overwhelming Brow, and Law-learn'd Face,
The Index of your Book of Common-place.

Thefe are mere Drudges, that can only plod,
And tread the Path their dull Forefathers trod,
Doom'd thro' Law's Maze, without a Clue, to range,
From *fecond Vernon* down to *fecond Strange*.
Do Thou uplift thine Eyes to happier Wits;
Dulnefs no longer on the Woolpack fits;
No longer on the drawling, dronifh Herd,
Are the firft Honours of the Law conferr'd;
But they, whofe Fame Reward's due Tribute draws,
Whofe active Merit challenges Applaufe,
Like glorious Beacons, are fet high to view,
To mark the Paths which Genius fhou'd purfue.

O for thy Spirit, *Mansfield!* at thy Name
What Bofom glows not with an active Flame?
Alone from Jargon born to refcue Law,
From Precedent, grave Hum, and formal Saw!
To ftrip Chican'ry of its vain Pretence,
And marry Common Law to Common Senfe!

Pratt! on thy Lips Perfuafion ever hung!
Englifh falls, pure as Manna, from thy Tongue:

On thy Voice Truth may reſt, and on thy Plea
Unerring *Henley* found the juſt Decree.

   Henley ! than whom to *Hardwicke*'s well-rais'd Fame,
No worthier Second Royal GEORGE cou'd name :
No Lawyer of Prerogative : no Tool
Faſhion'd in black Corruption's pliant School ;
Form'd, 'twixt the People and the Crown to ſtand,
And hold the Scales of Right with even Hand !

   True to our Hopes, and equal to his Birth,
See, ſee in *Yorke* the Force of lineal Worth ;
But why their ſev'ral Merits need I tell ?
Why on each honour'd Sage's Praiſes dwell ?
Wilmot how well his Place, or *Foſter* fills ?
Or ſhrew'd Senſe beaming from the Eye of *Willes ?*

   Such, while thou ſee'ſt the public Care engage,
Their Fame increaſing with increaſing Age,
Rais'd by true Genius, bred in *Phœbus*' School,
Whoſe Warmth of Soul ſound Judgment knew to cool ;
—With ſuch illuſtrious Proofs before your Eyes,
Think not, my Friend, you've too much Wit to riſe ;
Think of the Bench, the Coif, long Robe, and Fee,
And leave the Preſs to *Churchill*, and to *Me.*

THE

THE

MOUSE and OYSTER.

WHEN Midnight's fable Veil o'erfpread the
Plain,
When Bats and Fairies, Mice and *Morpheus* reign,
A bold undaunted Moufe that long defy'd
The various Stratagems that *Kate* had try'd,
His deftin'd Doom receiv'd ; for foon or late
Both Mice and Monarchs muft fubmit to Fate.

Oft was the Moon with Silver Luftre crown'd,
Since the nocturnal Pirate march'd his Round ;
Soon as his Foe, the Sun, had took his Flight,
Trips forth the little Champion of the Night ;
With cautious Tread, fecure from fell Mifhap,
Of Pufs, of Poifons or tremendous Trap,
Still at the Head of his rapacious Clan,
He fkipt from Shelf to Shelf, from Pan to Pan ;
With Nofe fagacious fmoak'd the baited Gin,
Wary and confcious of the Snare within :
Now feafts on rich Variety of Meats,
And oft in Cheefe his own Apartments eats ;
Regales on Floods of Cream, Ragouts, and Cakes,
Of all the Dainties of the Day partakes :

Now

Now ftorms rich Conferves with voluptuous Tafte,
And faps the tender Tenements of Pafte.
As yet unharm'd the Epicure patroll'd,
And fearlefs o'er his filent Suburbs ftroll'd ;
Luxurious Nights in pleafing Plunder pafs'd,
Nor dreamt that this was doom'd to be his laft.
For now the Time — the deftin'd Time was fent;
So Fate ordain'd — and who can Fate prevent ?
   Thick Shades once more had veil'd the haunted Houfe,
Once more from Coverts bolts th' adventrous Moufe,
Lighting in evil Hour in Queft of Prey,
Where in a Groupe th' avenging Oyfter lay :
A Fifh commiffion'd from the watry Throng,
With Ligament of fcaly Armour ftrong ;
Lay with expanded Jaws, and gaping Shell,
(But who the fad Cataftrophe can tell ?)
The dainty Moufe, ftill craving fome new Difh,
Enters the gloomy Manfions of the Fifh ;
With Beard exploring, and with lufcious Lip,
He longs the Pickle of the Seas to fip.
Rous'd by his Tufks, the elaftic Oyfter fell,
Caught clofe the Catiff's Head in watry Cell ;
In vain the Victim labours to get free,
From Durance hard, and dread Captivity :
Lock'd in the clofe Embrace, enfnar'd he lies,
In Pill'ry fafe, pants, ftruggles, fqueaks, and dies.

                           Thus

Thus the juſt Fate of his own Crimes he meets,
Like Rakes expiring in deſtruƈtive Sweets.

Now placed on high, the Maſter views the Prize,
And hails the Conqueſt with exulting Eyes!
And when beneath ſedate he ſits and ſmoaks,
And cracks his Nuts, his Bottles, or his Jokes,
His Tale he tells to grace the Chriſtmas Pye,
And to the trophy'd Relicks points on high.

TRANSLATION of an antient EPITAPH,
In the Cloyſters of *Winchefter College*.

E P I T A P H.

CLauſus Johannes jacet hic ſub marmore Clarkus,
Qui fuit hic quondam Preſbyter et Socius.
In terrâ Roſeos ſolitus ſtillare Liquores,
In cœlo vivis nunc quoque gaudet Aquis.

T R A N S L A T I O N.

BEneath this Stone lies ſhut up in the Dark,
A Fellow and a Prieſt, yclept *John Clark :*
With *earthly Roſe-water* he did delight ye,
But now he deals in *heavenly Aqua-vitæ.*

T H E

THE

NEW-YEAR's-GIFT.

Presented with a Pair of

SILK STOCKINGS,

To Miss Bell Cooke, of *Eton.*

I.

To please the Fair, in courtly Lays
    The Poet plays his Part,
One tenders Snuff, another Praise,
    A *Tooth-pick* or a *Heart.*

II.

Alike They all, to gain their End
    Peculiar Arts disclose,
While I, submissive, only send
    An *humble Pair of Hose.*

III.

Long may they guard from Cold and Harm,
    The snowy Legs that wear 'em,
And kindly spread their Influence warm
    To every Thing that's near 'em.

L   IV. But

IV.

But let it not be faulty deem'd,
  Nor move your Indignation,
If I a little partial feem
  In Gift or Commendation.

V.

Each fair Perfection to difplay
  Would far exceed my Charter;
My modeft Mufe muft never ftray
  Above the Knee or Garter.

VI.

And who did e'er a Bafis view
  So worthy to be prais'd?
Or from fo fair Foundation knew
  So fine a Fabrick rais'd?

VII.

Thou learned Leech, fage **** fay,
  Since fpite of Drugs and Plaifters,
You now can talk the live-long Day
  Of Pillars and Pilafters;

VIII.

You that for Hours have rov'd about,
  Thro' Halls and Colonades,
And fcarce would deign to tread on aught
  But Arches and Arcades;

IX. Did

IX.

Did you in all your mazy Round·
    Two nobler Pillars view?
What yielding Marble e'er was found
    So exquifitely true?

X.

The fwelling Dome with ftately Show
    May many Fancies pleafe;
I view, content, what lies below
    The Cornice and the Frieze.

XI.

The beauteous Twins, fo fair, fo round,
    That bear the noble Pile,
Muft fure proceed from *Venus' Mount*,
    Or from * *Cythera's Ifle.*

XII.

Propitious Fates, preferve 'em fafe,
    And keep 'em fnug together,
And grant they may the Malice brave
    Of Man as well as Weather.

* Two Places from whence the Ancients brought Materials for their moft noble Structures.

From

XIII.

From lucklefs Love, -or Rancour bafe,
　　May never Ill attend 'em ;
And grant, whatever be the Cafe,
　　That I may ftill defend 'em.

XIV.

By gentle, gen'rous Love, 'tis true,
　　They never can mifcarry ;
Nor Damage come, nor Lofs enfue,
　　From honeft, harmlefs *Harry*.

XV.

But fhould a Knight of greater Heat
　　Precipitate invade,
Believe me, *Bell*, they then may need
　　Some feafonable Aid.

XVI.

O may I ever be at Hand
　　From ev'ry Harm to fcreen 'em,
Then, *Samfon-like*, I'll take my Stand,
　　And live or die between 'em.

EXALTATION:

EXALTATION:

OR, THE

SIGNATURE of LOVE.

A DESCRIPTIVE PASTORAL.

In the *Modern* Style.

BEneath the Shadows of a glimmering Oak,
  Where confcious Meads in foft Delufion broke,
And ancient Murmurs, tremblingly awake,
Repel the neighbouring Coolnefs of the Brake;
Two Swains, reclining, footh'd th' enamour'd Tongue,
And thus with fragrant Vows, their Pipes they ftrung.

STREPHON.

In every Grove the various Floods combine;
A thoufand Beauties bafk upon the Line;
The folemn Breezes emulate the Day;
But Chloe is the Subject of my Lay.

CORYDON.

Let Thunder, fick'ning, fmile upon the Ground,
And mazy Beams reflect a dawning Sound;
Let lofty Echoes on Meanders throng;
But Phillis is the Burden of my Song.

STREPHON.

STREPHON.

Chloe's to me more fair than azure Sight;
More foft than Heifers melting into Light:
O come, ye Swains, and leave th' enamel'd Morn;
The moffy Garlands rival your Return.

CORYDON.

My Phillis, wond'ring, ftrives the Heat to pierce,
And fmiles precarious through the gay Reverfe:
Ye Hills and Dales that cheer the verdant Sand,
Bear me where Ages float at her Command.

STREPHON.

My Love, regardlefs of the vernal Main,
Like Honey blufhing, variegates my Pain;
And, like the Bee, fhe fmooths the mantled Green;
Soft as the Starts, and as the Hills ferene.

CORYDON.

My Love is like the rural Seats above;
The Canopy of Fate is like my Love;
My Love is like the Deep, in Purple dreft,
And all Ambrofia warbles in her Breaft.

STREPHON.

Now tell me, Corydon, and Chloe take,
What Thing is that, by Kings expell'd the Lake,
Whofe airy Footfteps faded as they grew,
Produc'd in Silence, yet alive in blue?

CORYDON.

CORYDON.

First tell me, Strephon, and be Phillis thine,
What Thing is that so daringly divine,
By Reason feather'd, and by Nature prest,
Refulgent, doubled, trebled, and unblest?

MENALCAS.

Enough, enough —— O Shepherds, your Delay
Retards the fleecy Partners of the Spray;
See, from yon Cloud impending Mirrors rise;
See how the Vallies wanton in the Skies!
From Wave to Wave reluctant Shades appear,
Revolving Swans proclaim the Welkin near,
And aid the breathing Surface of the Year.

EXTEMPORE LETTER

From Captain THOMAS *, at BERNERA, to Captain
PRICE, at FORT AUGUSTUS.

Written just before signing the Peace of Aix la Chapelle.

"COME, *Thomas*, give us t'other Sonnet,"
    Dear Captain, pray reflect upon it:
Was ever so absurd a Thing,
What, at the Pole, to bid me sing?

* Formerly Student of Ch. Ch. Oxford.

Alas!

Alas! fearch all thofe Mountains round,
There's no Thalia to be found;
And Fancy, Child of fouthern Skies,
Averfe the fullen Region flies ————

I fcribble Verfes? why you know,
I left the Mufes long ago;
Deferted all the tuneful Band,
To right the Files, and ftudy *Bland*.

Indeed in Youth's fantaftic Prime
Mifled, I wander'd into Rhyme,
And am'rous Sonnets penn'd in plenty,
On ev'ry Nymph, from twelve to twenty.
Compar'd to Rofes and to Lilies
The Cheeks of *Chloe* and of *Phillis*;
With all the Cant you'll find in many
A ftill-born modern Mifcellany.
My Lines, how proud was I to fee 'em,
Steal into *Dodfley*'s New Mufeum:
Or in a Letter Fair and Clean
Committed to the Magazine.
Our Follies change; that Whim is o'er,
The Bagatelles delight no more.
Know by thefe Prefents that in fine
I quit all Commerce with the Nine!

Love

Love-Strains, and all poetic Matters,
Lampoons, Epiftles, Odes, and Satires,
The Toys and Trifles I difcard,
And leave the Bays to Poet *Ward* *.

No, now to Politicks confin'd
I give up all the bufy Mind.
Curious, each Pamphlet I perufe,
And fip my Coffee o'er the NEWS;
But apropos, for laft Courant
Pray thank the Lady Gouvernante.
But what's this Rumour in the Mail
From *Aix* — pho, what is't, *la Chapelle?*
A Peace unites the jarring Pow'rs,
And ev'ry Trade will thrive but our's.
" Farewell, as wrong'd *Othello* faid,
" The plumed Troops, and neighing Steed."
The Troops, alas! more Havock there
A Peace will make, than all the War.
What Crowds of Heroes, in a Day,
Reduc'd to ftarve on Half their Pay!
From *Lowendahl* 'twould Pity meet,
And *Saxe* himfelf might weep to fee't.
Already Fancy's active Power
Fore-runs the near approaching Hour.

* An Officer in the fame Regiment.

Methinks

Methinks (curs'd Chance) the fatal Stroke
I feel, and feem already broke :
The Park I faunter up and down,
Or fit upon a Bench alone.
Sneaking and fad — le jufte portrait
D'un poŭvre Capitaine Reformé ;
My Wig, which fhun'd each ruder Wind,
Toupee'd before, and bagg'd behind,
Which *John* was us'd, with niceft Art,
To comb, and taught the Curls to part,
Loft the Belle-air, the jaunty Pride,
Now lank, depends on either Side.
My Hat, grown white and ruftick o'er,
Once bien troufsè with Galon d'Or.
My Coat diftain'd with Duft and Rain,
And all my Figure quite Campaign.
J'habillé fine with tarnifh'd Lace,
And Hunger pictur'd in my Face ;
Tavern or Coffee-houfe unwilling
To give me Credit for a Shilling ;
Forbid by ev'ry fcornful Belle,
The Precincts of the gay Ruelle.
My Vows, tho' breath'd in ev'ry Ear,
Not e'en a Chambermaid will hear ;
No Silver in my Purfe to pay
For Opera Ticket, or the Play.

No Meſſage ſent to bid me come
A Fortnight after to a Drum.
No Viſits or receiv'd or paid;
No Ball, Ridotto, Maſquerade.
All penſive, heartleſs, and chagrin,
I ſit devoted Prey to Spleen.

To you, dear *Price*, indulgent Heav'n
A gentler, happier Lot has giv'n;
To you has dealt, with bounteous Hands,
Palladian Seats, and fruitful Lands.
Then in my Sorrows have the Grace
To take ſome Pity of my Caſe,
And, as you know the Times are hard,
Send a ſpruce Valet with a Card;
Your Compliments —— and beg I'd dine,
And taſte your Mutton and your Wine;
You'll find moſt punctual and obſervant,
Your moſt oblig'd and humble Servant.

New-Market:

N E W - M A R K E T:

A S A T I R E.

Πουλυποvος ἱππεια,
Ος ἑμολες αιαιη
Ταδε γα.   Sophocl. Elect. 508.

H IS Country's Hope, when now the blooming
Heir,
Has loft the Parent's or the Guardian's Care ;
Fond to poffefs, yet eager to deftroy,
Of each vain Youth, fay, what's the darling Joy ?

Of

Of each rash Frolic what the Source and End,
His sole and first Ambition what ? —— to spend.

   Some 'Squires to *Gallia*'s Cooks devoted Dupes,
Whole Manors melt in Sauce, or drown in Soups:
Another doats on Fiddlers, till he sees
His Hills no longer crown'd with tow'ring Trees;
Convinc'd too late that modern Strains can *move*,
Like those of antient *Greece*, th' obedient Grove:
In headless Statues rich, and useless Urns,
Marmoreo from the classic Tour returns.——
But would ye learn, ye leisure-loving 'Squires,
How best ye may disgrace your prudent Sires;
How soonest soar to fashionable Shame,
Be damn'd at once to Ruin —— and to Fame;
By Hands of Grooms ambitious to be crown'd,
O greatly dare to tread *Olympic* Ground!

   What Dreams of Conquest flush'd *Hilario*'s Breast,
When the good Knight at last retir'd to Rest!
Behold the Youth with new-felt Rapture mark
Each pleasing Prospect of the spacious Park:
That Park, where Beauties undisguis'd engage,
Those Beauties less the Work of Art than Age;
In simple State where genuine Nature wears
Her venerable Dress of ancient Years;
Where all the Charms of Chance with Order meet
The Rude, the Gay, the Graceful, and the Great.

Here

Here aged Oaks uprear their Branches hoar,
And form dark Groves, which *Drui.'s* might adore;
With meeting Boughs, and deepening to the View,
Here fhoots the broad umbrageous Avenue:
Here various Trees compofe a chequer'd Scene,.
Glowing in gay Diverfities of Green:
There the full Stream thro' intermingling Glades
Shines a broad Lake, or falls in deep Cafcades.
Nor wants there hazle Copfe, or beechen Lawn,
To chear with Sun or Shade the bounding Fawn.

And fee the good old Seat, whofe *Gothic* Tow'rs
Awful emerge from yonder tufted Bow'rs;
Whofe rafter'd Hall the crowding Tenants fed,
And dealt to Age and Want their daily Bread;
Where crefted Knights with peerlefs Damfels join'd,
At high and folemn Feftivals have din'd;
Prefenting oft fair Virtue's fhining Tafk,
In myftic Pageantries, and moral Mafk.
But vain all antient Praife, or Boaft of Birth;
Vain all the Palms of old heroic Worth!
At once a Bankrupt, and a profperous Heir,
Hilario bets, — Park, Houfe, diffolve in Air.
With antique Armour hung, his trophied Rooms
Defcend to Gamefters, Proftitutes, and Grooms.
He fees his fteel-clad Sires, and Mothers mild,
Who bravely fhook the Lance, or fweetly fmil'd,.

All the fair Series of the whiſker'd Race,
Whoſe pictur'd Forms the ſtately Gallery grace;
Debas'd, abus'd, the Price of ill-got Gold,
To deck ſome Tavern vile, at Auctions ſold.
The Pariſh wonders at th' unopening Door,
The Chimnies blaze, the Tables groan no more.
Thick Weeds around th' untrodden Courts ariſe,
And all the ſocial Scene in Silence lies.
Himſelf, the Loſs politely to repair,
Turns Athieſt, Fiddler, Highwayman, or Play'r.
At length, the Scorn, the Shame of Man and God,
Is doom'd to *rub* the Steeds that once he *rode*.

Ye rival Youths, your golden Hopes how vain,
Your Dreams of Thouſands on the liſted Plain!
Not more fantaſtic *Sancho*'s airy Courſe,
When madly mounted on the magic Horſe *,
He pierc'd Heav'ns opening Spheres with dazzled Eyes,
And ſeem'd to ſoar in viſionary Skies.
Nor leſs, I ween, precarious is the Meed,
Of young Adventurers on the Muſe's Steed;
For Poets have, like you, their deſtin'd Round,
And Ours is but a *Race* on *claſſic Ground*.

Long Time, the Child of patrimonial Eaſe,
Hippolitus had carv'd Sirloins in Peace:

* *Clavileno.* See *Don Quixote*, B. ii. Chap. 41.

Had

Had quaff'd fecure, unvex'd by Toil or Wife,
The mild *October* of a private Life:
Long liv'd with calm domeftic Conquefts crown'd,
And kill'd his Game on fafe paternal Ground:
And, deaf to Honour's or Ambition's Call,
With rural Spoils adorn'd his hoary Hall.
As bland he puff'd the Pipe o'er weekly News
His Bofom kindles with fublimer Views.
Lo there, thy Triumphs, *Taaffe*, thy Palms, *Portmore*?
Tempt him to ftake his Lands and treafur'd Store.
Like a new Bruifer on *Broughtonic* Sand,
Amid the Lifts our Hero takes his Stand;
Suck'd by the Sharper, to the Peer a Prey,
He rolls his Eyes that " witnefs huge Difmay;"
When lo! the Chance of one inglorious Heat,
Strips him of genial Cheer, and fnug Retreat.
How awkward now he bears Difgrace and Dirt,
Nor knows the *Poor*'s laft Refuge, to be *pert*. ——
The fhiftlefs Beggar bears of Ills the worft,
At once with *Dulnefs* and with *Hunger* curft.
And feels the taftelefs Breaft *Equeftrian* Fires?
And dwells fuch mighty Rage in graver *'Squires?*
In all Attempts, but for their Country, bold,
Britain, thy CONSCRIPT COUNSELLORS behold;
(For fome perhaps, by Fortune favour'd yet,
May gain a Borough, from a lucky Bet,)

Smit

Smit with the Love of the *laconic* Boot,
The Cap, and Wig fuccinct, the filken Suit,
Mere modern *Phaetons*, ufurp the Rein,
And fcour in rival Race the tempting Plain.
See, fide by fide, his Jockey and Sir *John*
Difcufs th' important Point —— of *Six to One.*
For oh ! the boafted Privilege how dear,
How great the Pride, to *gain* a Jockey's *Ear !* ——
See, like a routed Hoft, with headlong Pace,
Thy *Members* pour amid the mingling *Race !*
All afk, what Crouds the Tumult could produce ——
Is *Bedlam*, or the *Commons* all broke loofe ?
Their Way nor Reafon guides, nor Caution checks,
Proud on a *high-bred Thing* to rifque their Necks.——
Thy *Sages* hear, amid th' admiring Croud
Adjudge the *Stakes*, moft eloquently loud :
With critic Skill, o'er dubious *Bets* prefide,
The low Difpute, or kindle, or decide :
All empty Wifdom, and judicious Prate,
Of *diftanc'd* Horfes gravely fix the Fate :
And with paternal Care unwearied watch
O'er the *nice Conduct* of a daring *Match.*

  Meantime, no more the mimic Patriots rife,
To guard *Britannia*'s Honour, warm and wife :
No more in Senates dare affert her Laws,
Nor pour the bold Debate in Freedom's Caufe :

Neglect

Negleft the Counfels of a finking Land,
And know no *Roftrum*, but *New-Market's Stand*.
 Is this the Band of Civil Chiefs defign'd
On *England*'s Weal to fix the pondering Mind ?
Who, while their Country's Rights are fet to Sale,
Quit *Europe's Ballance* for the *Jockey's Scale*.
O fay, when leaft their fapient Schemes are croft,
Or when a Nation, or a *Match* is loft ?
Who *Dams* ånd *Sires* with more Exaftnefs trace,
Than of their *Country's Kings* the facred Race :
Think *London Journies* are the worft of Ills ;
Subfcribe to *Articles*, inftead of *Bills :*
Strangers to all our *Annalifts* relate,
Theirs are the *Memoirs* of th' *Equeftrian* State :
Who loft to *Albion*'s paft and prefent Views,
HEBER *, thy *Chronicles* alone perufe.
 Go on, brave Youths, till in fome future Age,
Whips fhall become the *Senatorial Badge* ;
Till *England* fee her thronging Senators
Meet all at *Weftminfter*, in Boots and Spurs ;
See the whole *Houfe*, with mutual Frenzy mad,
Her Patriots all in Leathern Breeches clad :
Of *Bets*, not *Taxes*, learnedly debate,
And guide with equal Reins a *Steed* or *State*.

* Author of *an Hiftorical* LIST *of the Running Horfes*, &c.

How would a virtuous * *Houhnhym* neigh Difdain,
To fee his Brethren brook th' imperious Rein;
Bear Slavery's wanton Whip, or galling Goad,
Smoak through the Glebe, or trace the deftin'd Road,
And robb'd of † Manhood by the murderous Knife,
Suftain each fordid Toil of fervile Life.
Yet oh! what Rage would touch his generous Mind,
To fee his Sons of more than human Kind;
A Kind, with each exalted Virtue bleft,
Each gentler Feeling of the liberal Breaft,
Afford Diverfion to that Monfter bafe,
That meaneft Spawn of Man's Half-monkey Race;
In whom Pride, Avarice, Ignorance, confpire,
That hated Animal, a *Yaboo-Squire.*

How are the THERONS of thefe modern Days,
Chang'd from thofe Chiefs who toil'd for *Grecian* bays;
Who fir'd with genuine Glory's facred Luft,
Whirl'd the fwift Axle through the *Pythian* Duft.
Theirs was the *Pifan* Olive's blooming Spray,
Theirs was the *Theban* Bard's recording Lay.
What though the Grooms of *Greece* ne'er *took the Odds?*
They won no *Bets* — but then they foar'd to *Gods*;
And more an *Hiero*'s Palm, a *Pindar*'s Ode,
Than all th' united *Plates* of GEORGE beftow'd.

---

* *Vid.* GULLIVER's Travels. Voyage to the *Houhnhyms.*
† A Copy in the HARLEIAN Library reads HORSE-HOOD.

Greece?

Greece! how I kindle at thy magic Name,
Feel all thy Warmth, and catch the kindred Flame.
Thy Scenes fublime, and awful Vifions rife,
In ancient Pride before my mufing Eyes.
Here *Sparta*'s Sons in mute Attention hang,
While juft *Lycurgus* pours the mild Harangue;
There *Xerxes*' Hofts, all pale with deadly Fear,
Shrink at her fated ‡ Hero's flafhing Spear.
Here hung with many a Lyre of filver String,
The laureate Alleys of *Iliffus* Spring:
And lo, where rapt in Beauty's heavenly Dream
Hoar *Plato* walks his oliv'd *Academe.* ——

Yet ah! no more the Land of Arts and Arms,
Delights with Wifdom, or with Virtue warms.
Lo! the ftern *Turk,* with more than *Vandal* Rage,
Has blafted all the Wreaths of ancient Age:
No more her Groves by Fancy's Feet are trod,
Each Attic Grace has left the lov'd Abode.
Fall'n is fair *Greece!* by Luxury's pleafing Bane
Seduc'd, fhe drags a barbarous foreign Chain.

Britannia watch! O trim thy withering Bays,
Remember thou haft rivall'd *Grecia*'s Praife,
Great Nurfe of Works divine! Yet oh! beware
Left thou the Fate of *Greece,* my Country, fhare.

‡ LEONIDAS.

Recall thy wonted Worth with confcious Pride,
Thou too haft feen a *Solon* in a *Hyde* ;
Haft bade thine *Edwards* and thine *Henries* rear
With *Spartan* Fortitude the *Britifh* Spear ;
Alike has feen thy Sons deferve the Meed
Or of the moral or the martial Deed.

E P I T A P H

To the pie-houfe *Memory of* NELL BATCHELOR, *an*
Oxford Pye-Woman.

I.

HERE deep in the Duft,
The mouldy old Cruft,
Of *Nell Batchelor* lately was fhoven ;
Who was fkill'd in the Arts
Of Pies, Puddings, and Tarts,
And knew ev'ry Ufe of the Oven.

II.

When fhe'd liv'd long enough,
She made her laft Puff,
A Puff by her Hufband much prais'd ;
Now here fhe doth lie,
And makes a dirt Pye,
In hopes that her Cruft will be rais'd.

M 3   THE

THE

CASTLE BARBER's SOLILOQUY.

Written in the late WAR.

I Who with fuch Succefs — alas! till
The War came on — have *fhav'd* the *Caftle* ;
Who *by the Nofe*, with Hand unfhaken,
'The *boldeft Herces* oft have *taken* ;
In humble Strain, am doom'd to mourn
My Fortune chang'd, and State forlorn !

My

My *Soap* scarce ventures into Froth,
My *Razors* rust in idle Sloth!
WISDOM*! to you my Verse appeals;
You share the Griefs your *Barber* feels:
Scarce comes a *Student* once a whole Age,
To stock your desolated *College.*
Our Trade how ill an Army suits!
This comes of picking up *Recruits.*
Lost is the *Robber*'s Occupation,
No *Robbing* thrives — but of the *Nation:*
For hardy Necks no *Rope* is twisted,
And e'en the *Hangman*'s self is listed.——
Thy Publishers, O mighty *Jackson!*
With scarce a scanty Coat their Backs on,
Warning to Youth no longer teach,
Nor *live* upon a *Dying Speech.*
In Cassock clad, for want of Breeches,
No more the *Castle-Chaplain* preaches.
Oh! were our Troops but safely landed,
And every Regiment disbanded!
They'd make, I trust, a new Campaign
On *Henley*'s Hill, or *Campsfield*'s Plain:
Destin'd at Home, in peaceful State,
By me *fresh-shav'd*, to meet their Fate!

* The Governor of *Oxford Castle.*

Regard

Regard, ye Juſtices of Peace!
The CASTLE BARBER's piteous Caſe :
And kindly make ſome ſnug Addition,
To better his diſtreſt Condition.
Not that I mean, by ſuch Expreſſions,
To *ſhave* your *Worſhips* at the *Seſſions*;
Or would, with vain Preſumption big,
Aſpire to *comb* the *Judge's Wig* : ——
Far leſs ambitious Thoughts are mine,
Far humbler Hopes my Views confine. ——
Then think not that I aſk amiſs ;
My ſmall Requeſt is only this,
That I, by Leave of LEIGH or PARDO,
May, with the CASTLE — *ſhave* BOCARDO.
  Thus, as at *Jeſus* oft I've heard,
Rough Servitors in *Wales* preferr'd,
The *Joneſes, Morgans*, and *Ap-Rices*,
Keep *Fiddles* with their BENEFICES.

IMITATION.

IMITATION of HORACE.

Icci, beatis nunc Arabum invides
Gazis, &c.   L. I. Ode xxix.

SO you, my Friend, at laft are caught——
Where could you get fo ftrange a Thought,
   In Mind and Body found?
All meaner Studies you refign,
Your whole Ambition now to fhine
   The Beau of the Beau-monde.

Say, gallant Youth, what well-known Name
Shall fpread the Triumphs of your Fame
   Through all the Realms of *Drury?*
How will you ftrike the gaping Cit?
What Tavern fhall record your Wit?
   What Watchmen mourn your Fury?

What fprightly Imp of *Gallic* Breed
Shall have the Culture of your Head,
   (I mean the outward Part)
Form'd by his Parent's early Care
To range in niceft Curls the Hair,
   And wield the Puff with Art?

                              No

No more let Mortals toil in vain,
By wife Conjecture to explain
    What rolling Time will bring:
Thames to his Source may upwards flow,
Or *Garrick* fix Feet high may grow,
    Or Witches thrive at *Tring* :

Since you each better Promise break,
Once fam'd for Slov'nlinefs and *Greek*,
    Now turn'd a very *Paris*,
For Lace and Velvet quit your Gown,
The STAGYRITE for Mr. Town *,
    For *Drury-Lane* St. MARY's.

S   O   N   G.

GIVE Ear, and a comical Story I'll tell,
   'Tis of an old Doctor you know very well,
Who, tho' grave as a Saint, got as drunk as all Hell.
                Tol de rol, lol, &c.

It was on a Sunday, as all have agreed ;
For the Doctor he held it a Part of his Creed,
That the better the Day, the better the Deed.

* Author of the CONNOISSEUR.

He

He fat, and he drank, and he toafted old Cripfey,
But he never fufpected he e'er fhould grow tipfey,
He bung'd *cum feipfo* 'till he was not *feipfe.*

And when he had gotten as drunk as ten Bears,
He put on his Surplice, and ftagger'd down Stairs,
Tho' not able to fpeak, yet refolv'd to read Pray'rs.

· To the Defk then he came, and bow'd low on each Side,
I will rife and will go to my Father, he cry'd ;
But ftumbled and prov'd that he damnably lied.

To the Pfalms then he got, but would you know how,
He fpew'd on King *David*, and likely I trow,
For he was as drunk as was *David*'s old Sow.

To the Collects he got then, with much Hefitation,
While the Audience all were in great Expectation,
Inftead of a Pray'r came an Ejaculation.

And now with refpect to the Gown and the Band,
How bravely muft flourifh the Church of this Land,
Supported by Pillars not able to ftand!

                        Tol de rol, lol, &c.

EPITAPH

EPITAPH

ON

PARKER HALL,

Born and Executed at OXFORD.

HERE lies PARKER HALL, and what is more rariſh,
He was born, bred, and hang'd in St. Thomas's Pariſh.

EPIGRAM,

Occaſioned by Part of St. Mary's Church, *in* Oxford, *being converted into a* LAW SCHOOL.

YES, yes, you may rail at the *Pope* as you pleaſe,
But truſt me that *Miracles* never will *ceaſe.*
See here — an Event, that no *Mortal* ſuſpected !
See LAW and DIVINITY cloſely *connected !*
Which proves the old *Proverb* long reckon'd ſo odd,
That " the *neareſt* the CHURCH the *fartheſt* from
GOD."

V E R S E S

O F T H E

O X F O R D N E W S M E N,.

F R O M T H E

Year 1754 to the Year 1772.

THE
OXFORD NEWSMAN's VERSES,

For the Year 1754.

HAIL to this joyful Seaſon of the Year,
    Welcome alike to Ploughman and to Peer!
The buſy Houſewife with Domeſtic Cares
The ſweet Plumb-porridge and the Pie prepares:
Delicious Draughts the flowing Bowls afford,
And the fat Sur-Loin ſmokes upon the Board.
Now while your Hearts with generous Joys run o'er,
The neat-clad 'Prentice trips from Door to Door:
And can Ye to their Hands a Gift refuſe,
Who comb your Perukes, or japan your Shoes?
Now too, inſpir'd with Hopes of a Reward,
The BELLMAN ſpurns at Proſe, and ſoars a Bard:
While his ſlow Bell at Midnight Hour he chimes,
Streets, Lanes, and Allies ring with lofty Rhymes.
Shall not we NEWSMEN then, known Men of Letters,
Turn Poets at this Time to pleaſe our Betters?
Yet do not deem your Servants vainly bold,
Since many a Tale of others we have told,
If once in Verſe our Merits we unfold.

In

In Froſt, in Snow, in Tempeſt, and in Rain,.
Up the ſteep Hill, and o'er the miry Plain,
Patient we trudge ; nor e'er the Toils refuſe,
Sweltering with Noon-day Suns to bring you News..
Our weekly Sheets each Circumſtance relate,
And ſhew of JEWS and ‡ MARRIAGES the Fate.
From Us you learn what France and Spain deviſe,
From Us what Murders, Fires, Rapes, Robberies,.
Who wed, is born, is chriſten'd, or who dies.
This common Praiſe with others We inherit,
But We may plead to You ſuperiour Merit.
The various Feuds of INTEREST † OLD and NEW,
And who the *Green* upholds, and who the *Blue*,
We only can inform you ; cautious ſteering
In the vaſt Ocean of Electioneering.
    MASTERS ! howe'er inclin'd to our Petition,
Or *Green*, or *Blue*, oh ! make not Oppoſition.
We join no Party, praiſe not or revile,
Nor e'er perplex our Brains about the ‖ Style.
Reward our Labours, and but grant our Boon,
We ſhall not think that CHRISTMAS comes too ſoon.

‡ Alluding to the JEW and MARRIAGE Bills, which paſſed the preceding Seſſion. The firſt of theſe proved ſo unpopular as to be immediately repealed.

† The great Conteſt in Oxfordſhire was at this Time depending ; — and the Parties were reſpectively diſtinguiſhed by OLD and NEW INTEREST, or *Greens* and *Blues*.

‖ The Alteration of the *Style* had lately been under the Conſideration of Parliament.

VERSES, For the Year 1755.

THE hallow'd Seafon and the joyful Time,
   In which I us'd to greet you all with Rhyme,
Is now return'd —— to crown the Expectation,
Of thofe who follow the Mercurial Station :
Your Bounty then, which freely you impart,
Lives a whole Twelve-month in a grateful Heart;
Quickens our Steps and makes us fafter go,
And pay with Diligence what you beftow :
When Something of Importance 'tis we bring,
Your Goodnefs gives to every Heel a Wing :
Not Winds or Waters can impede our Way ;
Nor even Earthquakes can prolong our Stay.
Though *thofe*, we muft confefs, are *dreadful* Things !
And *LISBON*'s Defolation ‡ upward brings.
LISBON! that fhone about fome two Months fince,
Th' imperial City of a potent Prince ;
But now —— no more. Her Palaces are laid
As low as Earth, and almoft Atoms made.
Turrets that lately dar'd to brave the Sky,
Now undiftinguifh'd with the Rubbifh lye,
And can't pretend with Cottages to vie.

‡ The dreadful Earthquake at Lifbon.

        May

May Heaven defend us from fuch Evils *Here !*
And punifh Sin a little lefs fevere.
And, if we may extend a *Newfman*'s Prayers, ——
Confound the † *FRENCH*, and all their falfe Affairs!
That by *next Chriftmas* we may Carols fing,
To Peace and Plenty, Conqueft and *Our KING.*

V E R S E S, For the Year 1756.

A S longing Bridegrooms (join'd to heav'nly Fair)
Think Moments Months; each Minute a long Year;
Wifh the Day fpent, to make Exchange of Hearts,
When *Colin* kindly mutual Love imparts ;
Thanks the kind Gods who gave him *Phebe* fair,
Since all his Happinefs is centered *There.*
—— So long'd your NEWS-MAN for this joyous Tide
(For which Geefe fuffer, and the Pigs have cry'd)
That he may to his Cuftomers rehearfe,
In very humble, very home-fpun Verfe,
How the wild *Indians*, Savages forlorn !
(Virginia's Curfe, that ever fuch were born)
How they make Head ! — our Settlements difturb !
Till *Britain*'s rouz'd, their Infolence to curb.

† A War with France was now commenced.

But

But mark th' Event —— See *Washington* advance !
And *Winslow* || too ! —— that *Other Foe to France* !
— How *They Attack !* — Make a Retreat *more wise !*
And, PATIENT wait —— GREAT BRITAIN's *Known*
    Supplies.

    But what, good Sirs ! says honest *Ferdinando ?*
The *Bravest Men* can do — but what they can do :
All This was done — And, farther be it known,
If nought we've *gain'd*, we *hope* to save our own.

    On *Home Affairs* I'll not say much,
    (*My Paper* † gives 'em all a Touch)
There you will find who's *out*, or *in* ;
When the House rises ; when it sits again :
When Madam brings a darling Son ;
At Court — how *neatly* Things are done !
Who wants a Place, and *who* a Pension,
(*But these are Things I scarce dare mention*)
How some Folks rise, whilst others fall ;
Your *Newsman* brings Account of All :
Nor shall the *Patriot* be forgot,
The Man *who sits* ; or *who sits not* :
Advice in *This* is worth my Care ;
— I hope you'll LIKE *the Bill of Fare.*

    || Our Commanders in America, at this Time.
        † Oxford Journal.

                        But

But e'er I end, I beg you'll think
How far I've walk'd, with little Drink ;
How bad the Roads ! How cold the Weather !'
Two greater Ills can't meet together :
Yet pleafe to let me tafte your Bounty,
As heretofore, my Friend I'll count ye :
Then travel on (nor fear Difafters)
Till *CHRISTMAS* next, to ferve my Mafters.

VERSES, For the Year 1757.

WE NEWS-MEN, laft Week (you'd have laugh'd.
     had you feen us)
Met together thefe Verfes'to make up between us :
For we, like the Bellman, you know at this Seafon
Muft addrefs you in Verfe, though without Rhyme or
    Reafon.
Quoth * *Lochard*— for *Lochard*, (perhaps you mayn't·
    know it)
When infpired by Ale, is a very good Poet ——
" Shall we be dumb, while other Newfmen fing
" The glorious Deeds of *Pruffia*'s mighty King ?
" Shall we be dumb, when all who carry News.
" For || RAIKES or POCOCK, will this Subject chufe ;

* A very fingular Character, as a Newfman.
|| Printers of the *Gloucefter* and *Reading* Papers.

As

" As how in *Germany* he got the Day ;

" As how the King of *Poland* ran away.

" Shall we be dumb, when spite of General Blake-
ney,

" Minorca, || O Minorca !——*French* have
taken ye ?

" And shall not we lament the Price of Grain,

" We that have Mouths to eat, — and to complain ?"

Thus *Lochard* spoke in high heroic Rhymes :

Quoth another—— " But why must we talk of the
Times ?

" The Subject is stale, and our Verse only shews

" What *JACKSON* each Week has said better in
Prose.

" To move the kind Hearts of our Masters and
Mistresses.

" Let us talk of our own, not the National Distresses."

Then judge, my Mistresses, my Masters, judge,

What Hardships We endure, who patient trudge,

Through Wind and Wet, with scarce a Coat our
Backs on,

To bring you Journals every Week from
JACKSON.

|| General Blakeney commanded at Minorca, when that Place
was taken by the French in the Year 1756.

Weeks

Weeks *Fifty-one* without a Gift we've reckon'd :
O don't refufe us in the *Fifty-fecond !*
To your good· Healths, who let us have the Chink,
We Newfmen, as in Duty bound,- fhall drink.

V E R S E S, For the Year 1758.

ANOTHER Halfpenny upon NEWS-PAPERS !
Faith, 'twas enough to give us all the Vapours.
Our Mafter JACKSON vow'd it was a Sin,
And Nobody would take his Paper in.
To raife the Price he thought it was not right,
And he himfelf *net get a Farthing by't* ||.
Some Folks, he fear'd, would make it a Pretence
To leave his Journal off, and fave their Pence.
And yet he hop'd, you would not think it dear :
It is but *Two and Two-pence* in a *Year.*

Thanks to his Care, (and ours too, let me add)
We have as many Mafters, as we had :
Nay more, if you'll believe't — and where's the Wonder?
In Times fo full of Battles, Blood, and Plunder !
You Country Folks, that live fo far from Town,
And have no *London Papers* fent you down,

|| An Act had juft taken place for doubling the Duty or.
News-Papers.

Without

Without our JOURNAL never would have known
What's done in other Nations, and our own.
We told you, when our Fleet first fought the Main,
O Shame to ENGLAND! and came back again:
What the *Gazette* itself did never mention,
We told you of the *Hanover Convention**.
O for a Muse from OXFORD, whilst I sing
The glorious Deeds of PRUSSIA's Mighty King!
To tell the wond'rous Battles he has won:
But hold — this is too lofty — I have done. ——

    Though Master print his Papers ev'ry Week,
Did We not bring them, You would be to seek.
Think then, O think what Hardships we do bear,
What Toils we undergo throughout the Year,
With Pleasure we reflect on Troubles past,
And now rejoice, that CHRISTMAS comes at last.

VERSES, For the Year 1759.

LET *common* NEWSMEN common *Strains* indite,
  Alas! poor Souls, where should they learn to write?
But we of OXFORD boast superior Knowledge,
Where Learning flows from every Hall and College.

---

* The Convention of *Closter Seven*, in the Electorate of *Hanover*; in Consequence of which the late Duke of Cumberland
took Umbrage, and quitted the Army.

.Scholars indeed we know not, but are known
To moſt of thoſe that wait upon the Gown :
All vers'd in Arts, and deeply read in Books,
Bedmakers, Butlers, Manciples, and *Cooks :*
Oh could we learn from hence the happy Art,
To touch with Pity every Reader's Heart !
Now while each Journeyman and 'Prentice flocks,
For annual Favours, and a *Chriſtmas-Box,*
We beg the ſame ; attempting to repay
Our Maſters Bounties with an humble Lay :
Tho' paid in empty *Rhymes* the *Coin* excuſe,
No better *Coin* is current with the Muſe.

    Each vaſt Event our varied Page ſupplies,
The *Fall of* PRINCES, or the *Riſe of* PIES :
Patriots and *Squires* learn here with little Coſt
Or when a KINGDOM, or a MATCH is loſt ;
Both Sexes here approv'd Receipts peruſe,
Hence BELLES may *clean their Teeth,* — or BEAUX their
    Shoes.
From us inform'd, BRITANNIA's *Farmers* tell
How LOUISBOURG * by *Britiſh Thunder* fell ;
'Tis we that found to all the Trump of Fame,
And Babes liſp *Amherſt*'s and *Boſcawen*'s Name :

* Taken by General *Wolfe.*

The

The *Clerk* and *Sexton* ENGLAND's NAVY boaſt,
Denouncing Ruin to the *Gallic* Coaſt;
Glad Traders ſee the Fate of SENEGAL,
And CLIVE's new *Nabob* given to BENGAL;
Pruſſia's great Prince with Bumpers deep they hail,
While every Village quaffs it's *Chriſtmas Ale* :
All the four Quarters of the Globe conſpire
Our News to fill, and raiſe Your Glory higher;
While you ſit pleas'd each Enterprize to ſcan,
Which ARMS can execute, or PITT can plan.

VERSES, For the Year 1760.

THINK of the PALMS, my Maſters dear!
    That crown this memorable Year!
Come fill the Glaſs, my Hearts of Gold,
To BRITAIN's *Heroes* briſk and bold;
While into Rhyme I ſtrive to turn all
The fam'd Events of many a JOURNAL.
    FRANCE feeds her Sons on meager Soup,
'Twas hence they loſt their *Guardaloup* :
What tho' they dreſs ſo fine and ja'nty?
They could not keep *Marigalante.*
Their Forts in *Afric* could not repel
The Thunder of undaunted *Keppel*;

                       Brave

Brave Commodore ! how we adore ye
For giving us Succefs at *Goree.*
Ticonderoga, and *Niagara,*
Make each true *Briton* fing *O rare a!*
I truft the Taking of *Crown-Point*
Has put *French* Courage out of Joint.
Can we forget the timely Check
WOLFE gave the Scoundrels at ‡ *Quebec?* ——
That Name has ftopp'd my glad Career, ——
Your faithful *Newfman* drops a Tear! ——
  But other Triumphs ftill remain,
And rouze to Glee my Rhymes again.
  On *Minden*'s Plains, ye meek *Mounfeers!*
Remember *Kingsley*'s Grenadiers.
You vainly thought to *ballarag* us
With your fine Squadron off *Cape Lagos* ;
But when *Bofcawen* came, † *La Clue*
Sheer'd off, and look'd confounded blue.
† *Conflans,* all Cowardice and Puff,
Hop'd to demolifh hardy *Duff* ;
But foon unlook'd for Guns o'er-aw'd him,
HAWKE darted forth, and nobly *claw'd* him.

‡ Before this Place fell the brave *Wolfe*; yet with the Satisfac-
tion of firft hearing that his Troops were victorious. —The other
Places here enumerated were Conquefts of the preceding Year.
  † The French Admirals.

And

And now their vaunted FORMIDABLE
Lies Captive to a *Britiſh* Cable.
Would you demand the glorious Cauſe
Whence *Britain* every Trophy draws?
You need not puzzle long your Wit; ——
FAME, from her Trumpet, anſwers —— PITT.

VERSES, For the Year 1761.

WHILE each true *Briton* drops a Tear
    On GEORGE's * melancholy Bier,
Shall not we loyal Newſmen ſhew
Some Mark ſincere of ſocial Woe?
We that on Paper Wings on high
Have taught his Victories to fly,
Outſtripping e'en Imagination
To ſpread glad Tidings through the Nation;
When CANADA was made our own,
When PRUSSIA's Arms had conquer'd *Daun*;
Whene'er on Land we've Victors been,
Or gather'd Laurels on the Main.
    Thus though we juſtly boaſt of Merit,
We cannot ſhew a proper Spirit,

---

* GEORGE II. died in October 1760.

Unleſs

ｪUnleſs th' exhilarating Bowl
·Conſpires to warm the drooping Soul :
And drinking renders us unable
To cloath ourſelves in Coats of Sable :
Therefore, good Sirs, or Whig or Tory,
We beg to lay our Caſe before ye ;
And above all our worthy Maſters
We firſt addreſs the Pariſh Paſtors,
To give a caſt-off Suit for Mourning,
Of which we'll pay th' Expence of Turning;
So ſhall we Newſmen catch the Mode,
Nor trudge in Rags along the Road
As heretofore : — Hence Snow and Rain
Aſſault our hardy Limbs in vain.

And now, while ev'ry Table's found
With choiceſt Chriſtmas Dainties crown'd,
While you enjoy with wiſhful Eyes,
The rich Plumb-Pudding, Beef, and Pies,
Once more let's ſhare your gen'rous Treat,
With Money make our Purſe replete,
We'll bleſs the Bounty you afford,
And hail the Reign of G E O R G E the Third.

ｪV E R S E S.

VERSES, For the Year 1762.

WHILE JACKSON tells in Weekly Profe
How *Britain* triumphs o'er her Foes;
Your NEWSMAN comes, in Annual Rhymes
To paint the Glories of the Times:
And fure (nor think my Plan a low Whim)
Each Paragragh would make a *Poem*.

   Firft then, a foaming Tankard bring,
Sacred to GEORGE our youthful King;
Nor o'er your Newfman's Pipe and Pot,
Shall faireft CHARLOTTE be forgot;
Than whom (God blefs them!) more renown'd
A princely Pair were never crown'd!
Had I, poor Newfman, but been able
To fee them dine at *Lord May'r*'s Table,
I'm fure I fhould have ftrove and thruft hard
To carry off a fingle Cuftard.————
Come, all inferior Heroes ftand by,
For here's a Health to glorious *Granby*:
Whofe Cannons make moft noble Harmony
Amongft the poor *Mounfeers* in *Jarmony*:
But if his Name won't make ye fmile,
Think of our Trophies at *Belleifle*.

The

The *French*, from *Breſt*, about invading
Are always puffing and parading ;
Thoſe *Puffs* are all too weak, I doubt,
To *blow* their half-mann'd Navy *out*.
Come, let each *Engliſhman* be merry
At our ſubduing *Pondicherry*,
Whoſe Forts awhile ſtood ſhilly-ſhally,
'Till *Coote* was found too tough for *Lally*.
Sure, it deſerves of Punch a Sneaker,
To drink our Fleet at *Martineaker* ;
Which, if 'tis took, we hope to tip ye
The News of conquering *Miſſiſippi*.
Then ſoon all Threats of War will vaniſh
From Fleets and Armies, *French* or *Spaniſh*.
    Such are the Conqueſts *England* won
In the fam'd Year of Sixty-One.
'Twas then ſhe triumph'd, as ſhe ought ;
For, ſent by P I T T, her Heroes fought !

V E R S E S, For the Year 1763

T H E Peace is made at laſt —— *Heigh-ho !*
    The Folks above *would* have it ſo !
Sure they were mov'd with ſtrange Vagaries,
To ſign ſo ſoon PRELIMI-NARIES
'Tis mighty odd the Parliament
Should not petition *Our* Conſent.

We were in hopes, fince KEPPEL's Thunder
Had got the haughty *Spaniards* under,
That fome new Conqueſt would arrive
To make us hungry N E W S - M E N thrive;
And that another ſiege wou'd come,
To clothe our ſqualling Brats at Home.

   But fince upon our COLUMNS FOUR
We grave new Victories no more;
Since now *Blockades, Capitulations,*
Fleets, Countermarches, Camps, Invaſions,
By Sea, by Land, with many a Drub,
Amuſe no more the Weekly Club:
We muſt attempt to entertain
Your Fancies in another Strain: ——
Our Troops at *Portſmouth* ſafely landed,
And every Regiment diſbanded;
Thoſe Sons of *Mars* on HOUNSLOW's Plain
Will make, I truſt, a *new Campaign:*
Hence we new Paragraphs ſhall fetch
And ſhew you that great *General,* KETCH,
Leading his Heroes on to die
Without one Shrug, or Feature Wry.
We'll ſhew you many a *Country Village*
Left naked to the Soldier's *Pillage;*
Inſtead of *Towns,* where GRANBY thunder'd,
We ſhall exhibit —— *Henrooſts* plunder'd: ——
Look ſharp good Women, to your *Geeſe!* ——
Theſe are the bleſt Effects of *Peace!*

In fhort, whatever Paragragh
Shall make you cry, or make you laugh ;
'Tis your's to make your *Newfman* happy,
This Chiftmas, with a Cup of Nappy.

VERSES, For the Year 1764.

MY MASTERS all, we MEN of NEWS
Once more prefent our Yearly *Mufe* ;
Who tells you, with her ufual Lore,
What to expect in SIXTY-FOUR.
    What tho' with Trumpets, Drums, and Guns,
Your Ears no more our *Journal* ftuns,
We now fhall ope a new *Campaign*,
New bloody Wars —— on *Britain*'s Plain ;
Big with the Riots and the Routs
Of thofe fam'd *Chiefs* —— the I N S and O U T S:
Shall fhew you more furprifing Tricks
Of *Ambufcades* in Politicks ;
Th' *Attack*, *Retreat*, and *Countermarch*,
Of many a Politician arch.
But whether *Englifhman* or *Scot*
Should be Prime-Minifter or not ;
Whether our Paper pleas'd you moft
When PITT victorious *rul'd the Roaft* ;

Whether

Whether we beft fhall fhew our Duty
In drinking WILKES — or drinking BUTE t' ye;
'Tho' much is faid on either Side,
We take not on us to decide:
We NEWSMEN are of neither Party,
Alone for *England*'s Welfare hearty;
Impartial we record the *Fall*
Of *Rogues* and *Robbers* — *Great* and *Small*:
Nor BRITONS *North*, nor *South*, are We:
Our *Caufe* is G E O R G E and L I B E R T Y.

The *Bellman*, with his annual Rhyme,
Your Favour gains, this *Chriftmas* Time;
And fure you'll own, if Truth you tell,
In *Verfe* we N E W S M E N *bear the Bell.*

VERSES, For the Year 1765.

HARD Times indeed! — We Men of News,
    Who here prefent our *Yearly Mufe*,
Once hop'd our Poetry to raife,
When PEACE had fent us happier Days;
For PEACE, we thought, wou'd in her Train
Bring Plenty back to *Britain*'s Plain.——
A *Peace* d'ye call it ? — Sure 'tis worfe
Than even War's fevereft Curfe.

What's

What's the Advantage hence we reap?
Say, has it made *Provifions* cheap?
Scarce can we now *afford* to meet,
And fhare our annual *Sheep's Head Treat*.
Thefe Troubles are a grievous Tax on
The *Publifhers* of Mafter JACKSON.

Oh had we NEWSMEN rul'd the Helm,
While *Vict'ry* bleft this happy Realm,
Nor Spanifh *Dons*, nor French *Mounfeers*,
Had left all Parties by the Ears : ――
Our Peace had ftill been nam'd with Glory,
By growling *Whig*, and ranting *Tory* : ――
Not that we deem it meet to boaft,
Yet did we NEWSMEN *rule the Roaft*,
We'd fhew our Skill in Reformation,
Throughout the *Markets* of the Nation.

Meanwhile then, make *us Statefmen* happy
This Chriftmas with a Cup of Nappy :
Bring forth your Punch, your Strong, and Stale,
The fhiv'ring NEWSMAN's fure Regale :
Nor let the Authors of thefe Rhymes
Find your *Hearts* ― *harder* than the TIMES.

VERSES,

VERSES, For the Year 1766.

WHERE Captain Jolly's *House of Lords*
  At Eve a fnug Retreat affords,.
Amid the Clouds of many a Pipe,
Porter our Drink, our Supper Tripe,
Like folemn Minifters of State
We Newsmen held a grand Debate,
How beft, this Year, to entertain
The Public with a Chriftmas Strain ;
How beft to tell our noble Mafters
Of all our Dangers and Diftafters :
Each, o'er his Pint, propos'd his Plan ;
And thus the Confultation ran.

 Says *Bob*, a Politician bold,
" I think our Griefs might beft be told
" By fhewing, to the Nation's Ruin,
" What Mifchief Folks above are brewing :
" On Us thefe Ills are fure to fall,
" We helplefs Newsmen feel 'em all !
" *Enclofures*, and the *Cyder-Tax*,
" Have half already broke our Backs ;
" While all our future Hopes are vanifh'd
" Now William's dead, and Wilkes is banifh'd."

           Says

(212)

Says *Sam*, —— " My Lads —— our Pots, let's
 fill 'em ——

" And now you mention brave Duke WILL'EM,
" Suppofe, to better our Condition,
" The Country Parfons we petition,
" To give us, if they'll *tear* the Tuining,
" Their caft-off Coats to make us Mourning."
Says *Teague*, " Ay now by *Jafus*, *Honey*,
" If by your *Varfes* you'd get Money,
" Pray tell our Cuftomers, altho'
" 'Tis what *already* they muft know;
" That *Corn* is fo *extramely* dear,
" Our *Ale* is quite become *Small Beer* : —
" Sooner than thus I'll fpend my Penny,
" I'll join the *White-Boys* at *Kilkenny* ;
" Rather, while fuch Diftreffes wait us,
" I'd ftarve on *unexcis'd Potatoes*."
 While thus, uncertain what to fay,
We pafs'd the tedious Hours away,
And whiff'd our Pipes, and turn'd our Caxons,
Pop comes a *Devil* in from JACKSON's,
And threw thefe *Lines* before us down,
Sent by fome Poet of the *Gown*,
Who, tho' a Member of the *Varfity*,
Pities us in thefe Times of Scarcity.
" My Mafters kind, whom choiceft Liquors blefs,
" Reward your NEWSMAN's well-defign'd Addrefs!

        " Oh

" Oh think, how ill we fare, how oft we faſt,
" To whom *Sheeps-trotters* are a rich Repaſt!
" Regard our Wants, who travel cold and wet,   ...
" To crown your Breakfaſts with a Week's Gazette!
" Who, while the Snows deſcend, the Tempeſt roars,
" Convey the Fate of Nations to your Doors! ——
" Though JACKSON's weekly Pen our Paper frame,
" To us he owes One-Half of all his Fame;
" We lend a Hand to lift him to the Skies,
" And on our *Wings* abroad his JOURNAL flies."

VERSES, For the Year 1767.

DISMAL the News, which JACKSON's yearly Bard
    Each circling Chriſtmas brings, — " *The Times
    are hard!*"
There was a Time when *Granby*'s Grenadiers
Trimm'd the lac'd Jackets of the French Mounſeers;
When every Week produc'd ſome lucky Hitt,
And all our Paragraphs were plann'd by *Pitt.*
We Newſmen *drank* — as England's Heroes *fought,*
While every Victory procur'd — a *Pot.*
Abroad, we conquer'd France, and humbled Spain,
At Home, rich Harveſts crown'd the laughing Plain.

Then

Then ran in Numbers free the *Newfman's Verfes*,
Blythe were our Hearts, and full our Leathern Purfes.
But now, no more the Stream of Plenty flows,
No more new Conquefts warm the Newfman's Nofe.
Our fhatter'd Cottages admit the Rain,
Our Infants ftretch their Hands for Bread in vain.
All Hope is fled, our Families are undone ;
Provifions all are carry'd up to *London* ;
Our copious Granaries *Diftillers* thin,
Who raife our *Bread* — but do not cheapen *Gin*.
'Th' Effects of *Exportation* ftill we rue ; —
I wifh th' *Exporters* were *exported* too !
In every Pot-houfe is unpaid our Score ;
And generous *Captain* JOLLY ticks no more !
    Yet ftill in Store fome Happinefs remains,
Some Triumphs that may grace thefe annual Strains.
Misfortunes paft no longer I repeat ——
GEORGE has declar'd — that we again fhall *eat*.
Sweet *Willhelminy*, fpite of Wind and Tide,
Of Denmark's Monarch fhines the blooming Bride :
She's gone ! — but there's another in her Stead,
For of a Princefs Charlotte's brought-to-bed : —
Oh, cou'd I but have had one fingle Sup,
One fingle *Sniff*, at Charlotte's *Caudle-Cup !* —
I hear — *God blefs it* — 'tis a charming Girl,
So here's her Health in Half a Pint of Purl.

                                                  But

But much I fear, this Rhyme-exhaufted Song
Has kept you from your Chriftmas Cheer too long. —
Our poor Endeavours view with gracious Eye,
And bake thefe Lines beneath a CHRISTMAS-PIE!

VERSES, For the Year 1768.

STILL fhall the *Newfman's* annual Rhimes
Complain of *Taxes* and the *Times ?*
Each Year our COPIES fhall we make on
The Price of *Butter, Bread,* and *Bacon ?*
Forbid it, all ye Pow'rs of Verfe !
A happier Subject I rehearfe.
Farewell Diftrefs, and gloomy Cares !
A merrier Theme my Mufe prepares.
For lo! to fave us, on a fudden,
In fhape of Porter, Beef, and Pudding,
Though late, ELECTIONEERING comes! ———
Strike up, ye Trumpets, and ye Drums !
At length we change our wonted Note,
And feaft, all Winter, on a Vote.
Sure, Canvaffing was never hotter !
But whether *Harcourt, Nares,* or *Cotter* †,

† Candidates for the City of Oxford.

At

At this grand Crisis will succeed,
We *Freemen* have not yet decreed.——
Methinks, with Mirth your Sides are shaking,
To hear *Us* talk of *Member-Making!*
Yet know, that *We* direct the State ;
On *Us* depends the Nation's Fate. —
What though some *Doctor's* cast-off Wig
O'ershades my Pate, not worth a Fig ;
My whole Apparel in Decay ;
My Beard unshav'd — on *New-Year's Day* ;
In me behold, (the Land's Protector)
A *Freeman, Newsman,* and *Elector!*
Though cold, and all unshod, my Toes : —
My Breast for *Britain's* Freedom glows : —
Though turn'd, by Poverty, my Coat,
It ne'er was turn'd to give a Vote.

Meantime, howe'er improv'd our Fate is
By jovial Cups, each Evening, *gratis* ;
Forget not, 'midst your *Christmas* Cheer,
The Customs of the coming Year : ——
In answer to this short Epistle,
Your Tankard send, to wet our Whistle !

VERSES,

VERSES, For the Year 1769.

WE *Men* of *News*, in former Days,
  Had glorious Subjects for our Lays :
The *Mutton-Pies* * of witty BEN
Employ'd, each Year, our constant Pen ;
And oft our *Christmas Carol* sung
The joint Renown of JOLLY YOUNG. —
Such were the Newfman's Strains of yore !
But *Mutton-Pies* are now no more :
And (Theme too high for humble Writer)
Lo ! CAPTAIN JOLLY keeps the *Mitre*.
Meantime, our Soldiers and Commanders
Sent us brave Paragraphs from *Flanders* ;
And oft our *Tars*, for Conquest eager,
Prov'd Beef superior to Soup-meagre :
While into Rhyme we strove to turn all
The fam'd Events of many a JOURNAL.
Our Poets too, ne'er known to flinch,
Who help'd us often at a Pinch, •
(Though brisk and merry once as *Griggs*)
Are now grave *Dons* in grizzle Wigs. —

* See p. 17, et seq.

And

And is there now no rifing W I T
With Love of Verfe and Porter fmit ?
No *Frefhman* intimate with J A C K S O N
Whom we may lay this annual Tax on ?
Ah! what, my M A S T E R S, can we do,
Our *Subjects* loft, and *Poets* too ! —
Subjects there are, I grant ye, ftill,
But all above our grey-goofe Quill :
The Vifit of the *Royal Dane* *,
The Travels of the *Northern Thane* ||,
Queen C H A R L O T T E's happy *Lying-in*,
The Trophies of triumphant G L Y N N §,
Our *Patron* W I L K E S, in Durance vile,
Demand a more exalted Stile. ——

What then, to clofe our Song, remains ?
But that, in unambitious Strains,
We fend a Wifh, that jovial Cheer
May ufher in the coming Year ;
That Peace and Plenty both agree
To make us honeft, rich, and free :
To wipe away (as heretofore)
The *Nation's* and the *Newfman's* Score :
That Fortune's faireft Rays may fhine
To gild the Dawn of S I X T Y - N I N E.

* King of *Denmark.* || Lord Bute.   § Elected.

V E R S E S,

VERSES, For the Year 1770.

A S now *Petitions* are in Fashion
    With the first Patriots of the Nation ;
In Spirit high, in Pocket low,
We *Patriots* of the *Butcher-Row*,
Thus, like our Betters, ask Redress
For high and mighty *Grievances*,
Real, tho' penn'd in Rhyme, as those
Which oft our JOURNAL gives in Prose : ——

   " Ye rural Squires, so plump and sleek,
" Who study — JACKSON, once a Week ;
" While now your hospitable Board
" With cold Sirloin is amply stor'd,
" And old October, nutmeg'd nice,
" Send us a Tankard and a Slice !
" Ye Country Parsons, stand our Friends,
" While now the driving Sleet descends !
" Give us your antiquated Canes,
" To help us through the miry Lanes ;
" Or with a rusty Grizzle-Wig
" This Christmas deign our Pates to rig.
" Ye noble Gem'men of the *Gown*,
" View not our *Verses* with a Frown !

                    " But

" But, in return for *quick Difpatches,*

" Invite us to your Buttery-Hatches !

" Ye too, whofe Houfes are fo handy,

" For Coffee, Tea, Rum, Wine, and Brandy ;

" Pride of fair Oxford's gawdy, Streets,

" You too our Strain fubmiffive greets !

" Hear *Horfeman, Spindlow, King,* and *Harper!* * —

" The Weather fure was never fharper : —

" Matron of Matrons, MARTHA BAGGS !

" Dram your poor *Newfman* clad in Rags !

" Dire Mifchiefs Folks above are brewing,

" The *Nation's* — and the *Newfman's* Ruin : —

" 'Tis Your's our Sorrows to remove ;

" And if thus generous ye prove,

" For Friends fo good we're bound to pray

" Till — next returns a *New Year's Day !*"

   " *Giv'n at our melancholy Cavern,*

   " *The Cellar of the* SHEEP'S-HEAD TAVERN."

VERSES, For the Year 1771.

Delicious News — *A War with Spain !*
   New Rapture fires our Chriftmas Strain.
Behold, to ftrike each *Briton's* Eyes,
What bright victorious Scenes arife !

* Keepers of noted Coffee-Houfes in *Oxford.*

What

What Paragraphs of *Englifh* Glory
Will Mafter JACKSON fet before ye!
The Governor of *Buenos Ayres*
Shall dearly pay for his Vagaries;
For whether *North*, or whether *Chatham*,
Shall rule the Roaft, we muft have-at-'em:
Galloons — *Havannah* — *Porto Bello*, —
Ere long, will make the Nation mellow: ———
Our late trite Themes we view with Scorn,
Bellas the bold, and Parfon *Horne:*
Nor more, through many a tedious Winter,
The Triumphs of the Patriot *Squinter*,
The *Ins* and *Outs*, with Cant eternal,
Shall croud each Column of our JOURNAL. —
After a dreary Seafon paft,
Our Turn to live is come at laft:
Gen'rals, and *Admirals*, and *Jews*,
Contractors, *Printers*, MEN OF NEWS,
All thrive by *War*, and line their Pockets,
And leave the Works of *Peace* to Blockheads.
    But ftay, my Mufe, this hafty Fit —
The War is not declar'd as yet:
And we, though now fo blythe we fing,
May all be *prefs'd* to ferve the King!
Therefore, meantime, our MASTERS dear,
Produce your hofpitable Cheer: —

While

While we, with much fincere Delight,
(Whether we publifh *News* — or fight)
Like *England*'s undegenerate Sons,
Will drink — *Confufion to the* Dons !

VERSES, For the Year 1772.

WHILE We full fadly labour through the Winter,
How nobly thrives our Journal's honour'd
Printer !
A lucky Dog, and born to fave his Bacon,
Behold, the *King's-head Tavern* he has taken !
There with *new Almanacks* he cuts a Flafh,
And lines with many a *Mag.* th' extended Safh.
What though, as if the Houfe had ftill a Sign,
His Cellar's ftor'd with Brandy, Rum, and Wine,
In fuch rich Draughts our Cares We feldom drown —
He keeps them — for his *Authors* of the *Gown*.
Correctors, Puffers, Paragraph-compofers,
Scribblers, and Scribes, your Poets and your Profers,
Lo, thefe (fo crofs of human Things the Fate is!)
Each Eve frequent our Mafter's Tavern *gratis:*
While We who lend his Journal Wings to foar,
Higher than Journal ever flew before,
Our Spirits down, our Wigs without a Curl,
Can fcarce procure a fcanty Pint of Purl.

Yet

Yet ftill fome Hopes of future Luck remain
In ftore -- Methinks I fpy a War with *Spain*.
JACKSON! too long thy Journal has been full
Of Jews, of Ducheffes, of *Wilkes* and *Bull*;
And fure, although I think he feems to tune us,
We've had enough of that fly Rafcal *Jun'us*:
A War wou'd give new Spirit to our Paper,
And make our *Mafter* and his *Newfmen* caper.

But let us look at Home — and Fortune there
A more propitious Afpect feems to wear :
The *Paving-Act* though many a Poor Man rues,
It brings fome Comfort to us *Men of News*:
Rare Tidings for the Wretch whofe lingering Score
Remains unpaid — BOCARDO * is no more !
Nor more, where many a *Publifher* has ftood,
The PILLORY * uprears its Yoke of Wood :
Nay ev'n the STOCKS, * where, having quaff'd our Fill,
We fate in State, have left the *City-hill :*
To crown the Whole, and what you all muft know,
The HANGMAN was enlifted long ago †.

Yet ah! mid real Sorrows and Vexations,
How vain are all fuch flattering Confolations !

* The City Goal, &c. taken down by the *Oxford* Paving Act.
† See p. 183.

Can

Can *Hopes* of happier Times our Wants remove ?
A *prefent* Help can *Expectation* prove ?
Therefore, my Mafters, your Relief afford,
Nor fhut the *Newfman* from your *Chriftmas* Board !
Your Bounty yet was never known to fail us,
Come then, as ufual, dram us, punch us, ale us;
And, not averfe to this our Song's Defign,
At leaft permit us once a Year to DINE.

F I N I S.

www.ingramcontent.com/pod-product-compliance
Lightning Source LLC
Chambersburg PA
CBHW030127030726
47498CB00007B/2580